I've Got A Crush On You.

CAROL STANLEY

SCHOLASTIC BOOK SERVICES
New York Toronto London Auckland Sydney Tokyo

For Doug

Cover Photo by Owen Brown

ISBN 0-590-30324-4

12 11 10 9 8 7 6 5 4 3 2 1   8   0 1 2 3 4 5/8

Printed in the U. S. A.   06

I've Got A Crush On You.

A Wildfire Book

WILDFIRE TITLES

Love Comes to Anne by Lucille S. Warner
Christy by Maud Johnson
That's My Girl by Jill Ross Klevin
Beautiful Girl by Elisabeth Ogilvie
Superflirt by Helen Cavanagh
Just Sixteen by Terry Morris
Suzy Who? by Winifred Madison

1

"You think you can find another girlfriend for rainy nights?" Beth asked Matt.

"What do you mean?"

"I don't think the top on this thing is real watertight. I'd be willing to let someone else get drizzled on."

They were sitting in the ancient MG Matt had bought the week before, being pulled along — by a chain attached to the front bumper — through the Speedee Car Wash on the corner of Elm and Bryant. A steady trickle of water was running down the inside of the door on Beth's side.

"I guess you'll just have to snuggle up closer to me," Matt said.

"I think just sitting in a car this small qualifies as snuggling."

"Oh, no!" he cried. "The Attack of the Giant Roller Brush!" He let out a fake scream and grabbed Beth as if to protect her from the roller brush that was indeed at that moment rolling up the hood of the car toward the windshield.

After being rinsed and dried and hot-waxed and buffed, they came out of the cinder block tunnel into the light of one of the last days of Indian Summer to linger in Danube, Illinois, that year.

"Top down?" he asked her.

"That's what you bought it for, isn't it, to feel the wind through your hair and the envious eyes of pedestrians upon you?"

"Actually, I thought it might help me attract the right sort of girl, the kind who doesn't make fun of me so much."

"I know a couple of nice, meek ones," Beth told him. "I'd be glad to fix you up."

She knew she was safe, that — teasing and all — Matt would rather be out with her than with any other girl at Hamilton High. Which was a nice, secure feeling. To have someone completely devoted to you. Of course, she worried sometimes that it was wrong to let a boy feel this way about you when you couldn't return it in the same degree. Several months ago he had given her a signet ring. This was on their fourth date, before she was even sure she liked him, but she kept it because she couldn't think of how to turn down something that someone had already had monogrammed and couldn't take back. Now she knew she liked him fine, but was beginning to be sure it wasn't ever going to heat up any more than where it was now.

A few weeks ago, she had asked Sandy if she thought this was a problem. Sandy, by virtue of being hyperactive and in possession of two very permissive parents, had been dealing with boys since she was eleven and by now had her expert badge.

"Just don't lie."

"I don't think I'm that type. I mean, isn't that sort of thing reserved for girls who go after guys they meet at roulette tables?"

"No. Sometimes you can even be a clean, upstanding, adolescent member of a conventional Midwestern community and still get done in by circumstances."

"Like?"

"Like you go for a walk in the forest on one of those beautiful August days when the sun's so bright, it almost, but not quite, makes it through the heavy leaves above you and makes everything smell unbearably green, and he kisses you and says he loves you, and because you feel you ought to respond in kind or because you want to make the moment significant, you tell him you love him too."

"Oh, we've already been through that pass."

"And?"

"And I told him I didn't feel that strongly about him. But what bothers me is that I didn't tell him I probably never would."

"No one expects you to be a fortuneteller. Just so you like him now and make it clear it's only liking."

"Well, I do like him. Sometimes a lot. It's been a real easy time for me with him. It feels sort of nice and drifty. Especially after last year with all those fights with Bob, and my parents on my back all the time, and waking up every morning not having any idea what the weather inside me was going to be like that day. This year I feel like everything has sort of fallen into place and that Matt's part of all that."

"Must be nice to have everything knocked at seventeen."

"Come on." Beth had blushed for having sounded so smug. Still, it was hard not to be, just a little. Things *were* going awfully well for her lately. She liked her classes this year, and that was showing in her grades. She was pretty sure she wouldn't have any trouble getting into a good college. And, so far, senior year — with everybody having known each other so long and getting already a little misty about breaking up the set — had a sort of party atmosphere to it. And Matt seemed like the right guy to be at a party with.

With the sun gleaming off the hood of the MG and the smell of dying leaves in the air, Beth and Matt drove out of town a ways, into the surrounding farmland. He drove with great concentration on taking the curves of the road tightly, shifting through the gears smoothly. She could tell he was in the throes of a love affair with this, his first car. His preoccupation gave her a chance to look at him closely, something she liked to do when she had a chance.

Mostly, she guessed, he looked like the jock he was. He was big, with big hands that looked right gripping a bat or passing a football, but were slightly oversized holding on to the steering wheel of a small, foreign sports car. He had cheeks that were perpetually reddened, even indoors, and hair that was a mixture of blond and brown, straight and thick, and usually falling into his eyes. He had a wide, open, middle-American face, a Norman Rockwell kid grown up. He didn't look like and probably wasn't a person of great depth. He had a life neatly planned for himself. He had already applied and been accepted to a small college in the western part of the state, where they had a good business administration program. Afterward he was going to work for his father in the insurance business. She could see him in fifteen years as the kind of guy who played the father in one of those family TV shows. The problem was that, more and more, she could not see her own future resembling anything she saw on TV.

2

No one was in Beth's house when Matt dropped her off around six-thirty. When she was little, the few times she had come home from grade school and been unable to find somebody in the house right away had made her desperate with the fear that her family had moved away. Now that she was almost an adult, now that she was a mature and reasoning person, she only panicked that they had all gone on vacation without her.

She found them — her mother and father and Harry — in the backyard having a cookout. Now that the sun had gone down, the summer had gone out of the day, and everyone was sitting at the picnic table in jackets. They all looked up when she came out through the back door.

"We eat at six around here," Beth's father

said, holding in his hands a large, floppy hamburger with a loose tomato slice sliding out of one side.

"Matt wanted to blow out the pipes on the new car, so we drove all the way out to Landis and back."

"I'm not interested in Matt's automotive needs. I'm concerned that we eat at least one meal a day together as a family." He put his hamburger down and spread his hands to encompass the scene around him. "This is a fantasy I used to have — that I'd get to grill the burgers and sit at the head of the table with all my kids around me. I mean, if I don't get a few pay-offs like that, it's going to start me thinking, why didn't I stay a swinging bachelor. Which I was, you know. Incredibly swinging."

"I hope you kids aren't paying any attention to this," Beth's mother said. "When I met him, he used to stay in Saturday nights and eat TV dinners at this little table facing the wall. We saved him from all that."

"Arg," her father said and leaned over to fake-bite Beth's mother on the arm.

Beth thought her parents were — aside from everything else good or bad — very funny. She knew lots of other kids' parents weren't and figured she had a real advantage here. She was sorry, at moments like this, that their good humor was lost on Harry, who since he turned thirteen had decided to be a professional jerk.

"Can I have a hamburger?" Beth asked. Then added, "Or two?" to be on the safe side.

She was always hungry these days. She knew she had started to gain weight. Even though she avoided the bathroom scale, she could tell by how tight her clothes were beginning to fit.

"Can you say you're sorry for being late?" her father asked. "I'm still feeling angry with you for spoiling this cook-out with your absence, and if you don't apologize, I'll have to express this anger in a healthy way. Healthy for me, that is."

"I'm sorry for being late," Beth said in a hurry. In the few months that her dad had been going to a psychiatrist, he had been talking like this — straight-on and open. On the one hand, it embarrassed Beth. It wasn't the way fathers were supposed to talk. On the other hand, it was kind of nice. She always knew what was going on with him. And it made her feel good to be talked to so honestly. And so she tried to be worth it, to act, at least around him, like the adult he seemed to assume she was.

"Why don't you put the burgers on yourself?" he suggested. "They're all made up over there on the table next to the grill. The coals are pretty low now, so it might take a while. Why don't you put them on, then go upstairs and get a jacket."

"Why *are* we eating outside anyway?" she asked.

"We thought we'd try to hold off the fall," her mother said, "but it doesn't look like we're one hundred percent successful."

"You're all nuts, you know," Beth yelled over her shoulder as she ran inside to get her parka.

"And it's probably hereditary," her mother called after her.

When she came back out, her hamburgers were ready to turn over and her brother Harry was waiting to sell her out.

"You know," he said, drawing the words out into a whine. Beth had just sat down at the table with her plate, so she knew whatever he was about to say would have to do with her and would be pukey.

"You know," he repeated, in case he didn't have everyone's full attention, "Rick James was riding his bike past the car wash this afternoon and saw Beth and Bozo cruising through like it was the Tunnel of Love." Harry never called Matt anything but Bozo. Unfortunately, her family had picked it up — not maliciously, just sort of in fun. Which made Beth nervous when she brought Matt around. She was afraid one of them would forget and let it slip out.

"That sounds like it might be dangerous," was all her mother had to say about the car wash incident.

"I think it might be one of those things that sounds dangerous, but is really just dopey. You don't do it every day, do you? You don't get strange urges in the middle of the night to go down there for a quick wash?" her Dad asked.

"Of course not." There was nothing she could say that wouldn't get her in deeper, or at least inspire more teasing. It was clearly one of those things that seemed cute in the doing and incredibly stupid in the retelling. Especially in Harry's version.

She was trying so hard to present a new image to her parents lately. She wanted them to think of her as competent and sensible and mature and trustworthy.

She could kill Harry. She tried to tell herself he was like this because he was so miserable inside himself. She reminded herself that he was pimply and friendless and insecure and was constantly being picked up for stealing really dumb stuff like paint rollers and pinking shears. Sometimes, in rare moments of detachment and generosity, she could even work herself up to feeling sorry for him. But mostly, she just wanted to kill him.

"I could kill you, you know," she told him later that night. He was standing in the bathroom in his pajama bottoms, carefully applying the latest in a long series of creams prescribed for him by Dr. Davis, his dermatologist.

"I'm really scared," he said, without turning from the mirror.

"You know, other brothers and sisters have codes of honor. They don't rat on each other."

"I wasn't ratting. I just find you amusing. Everyone around here is always telling me I don't contribute enough to the general conversation. So tonight I had a little anecdote and you don't appreciate it." He sighed theatrically. "I guess one can't please everybody."

One of the things about Harry that really drove Beth nuts lately was that he talked like this most of the time. It seemed to be a bad imitation of the tennis-playing playboy character — the one who always turns out to be involved in the seamy blackmail plot — in the old movies he watched on the *Late Show*.

By the time she got to her room, she felt bad. She always hated herself for letting Harry get her down to his level. Sometimes she wished she and Harry could start over, go back two or three years to before all this friction had started, to the old days when they had been close and liked each other and shared secrets.

She still wasn't sure what had gone wrong. A lot of it was probably her fault. Telling him to get lost when he was being a pest. Maybe those were the times he had really needed her to give him some important advice, or just needed her to be around.

Other times, it seemed like he was disgusted with everybody and it didn't have much to do with her in particular. Her mother told Beth not to pay much attention to Harry, that he was "hormonally out of whack." She knew this was probably true and yet it wasn't a particularly helpful piece of information in the daily waiting forever for him to get out of the bathroom. And having conversations in which, even if she was trying, he was only in them to put her down.

She went to sleep thinking there probably wasn't any fast solution to the Harry problem. All she could come up with was the chicken way out of avoiding him until she thought of a new approach.

3

Beth was sitting in World History listening with amazement to Alice Cullen talk about the culture of the Phoenicians. Everyone made fun of Alice Cullen, with her mismatched socks and grade-school pencil case with bunnies and duckies on it. And everyone hated how she "helpfully" corrected anybody who gave a wrong answer, and how she raised her hand for nearly every question.

But at times like this, Beth — who knew that Phoenicia was somewhere near the Mediterranean and that was about it — was glad there was someone around to take the heat off her. By the time Alice got done spouting off everything she knew about the Phoenicians, there wouldn't be any questions left for Miss Aldrich to ask, and everyone would be off the hook. You had to hand it to Alice in a way. She must, Beth suspected, even find extra books in the library on the subject, and not just the encyclopedia. At any rate, the stuff she knew wasn't in the textbook, which is as far as Beth would have thought to look.

Sometimes Beth thought about becoming a Cullenlike whiz — spending Saturday afternoons at the library doing independent research projects, underlining all her textbooks, and organizing her class notes into handy three-by-five cards so that the night before a test, all she'd have to do was review everything for an hour or so, then have a cup of cocoa and go to bed. She bet Alice Cullen was heavily into cocoa.

For Beth, nights before tests were coffee-jazzed marathons of desperately trying to stuff six weeks of material into six hours. This worked often enough to give her a B average, but it was more like playing a game — passing meant winning — than like the "quest for knowledge" all her principals since first grade had talked about in their orientation speeches.

The only work she got that kind of pleasure from, enjoyed doing for its own sake, was writing poems. She took out of her sweater pocket a looseleaf sheet creased in four—the poem she was working on now. It was about school.

She looked up. Alice was still going on. By now she was on to agricultural achievements of the Phoenicians. It really was amazing.

Except for Miss Aldrich, no one else seemed impressed. Vince Bugati was the only one who even looked like he was paying attention, but since he was almost world famous for his talent of sleeping with his eyes open, when he looked like he was paying attention it usually meant he was sound asleep. Which was a lot of the time now that he worked several nights a week in his uncle's restaurant.

Bev Wyatt, who got a lot of good, back-of-the-room seats because of her last name being at the end of the alphabet, was giving herself a manicure. She always wore a shade of polish called Fashion Orchid because, she had told Beth, her mother thought it made her look like a corpse. They weren't getting along and the nail polish was one of Bev's maneuvers in their ongoing warfare.

Yvette Kramer was looking through her wallet for the five millionth time at pictures of her boyfriend, who was in college. The dopey thing about these photos was that they had all been taken on the same day at the beach last summer. They were different from each other only in that in one the boyfriend would be facing a little more this way, in another a little more that way. He was also, in Beth's opinion, not very cute, but to watch Yvette flip through those pics, you'd think she was watching a Robert Redford movie.

Ed Schultz was reading a sci-fi comic book he had hid under his notebook. Pam Patterson was doing her calculus homework. Don Frey was drawing an anchor on the back of his hand. He had been doodling like this — on himself, or his desk top, or on the back of whoever was sitting in front of him — for as long as Beth had been in classes with him, which was as long as she could remember, maybe as far back as first grade. She still couldn't tell whether this meant he was a burgeoning artist, or a little simple.

It was not a class at peak attention. This would change when the Alice Cullen Show came to a close and Miss Aldrich took over again. She was actually a pretty good teacher, Beth thought. She traveled a lot over summer vacations and took slides of ancient stuff and knew what she was talking about and made it interesting. Egypt had been the best so far.

Beth was also especially interested in Miss Aldrich since the night last month when the family had gone out to dinner for Harry's birthday at the Flaming Spit restaurant out on 41. After they got seated, Beth had looked around and there at a table in the back was Miss Aldrich, holding hands with some guy, with a bottle of wine in a silver ice bucket next to them. The two of them left soon after Beth arrived, so she didn't really have a chance to study the details of the situation.

She knew it was ridiculous to be shocked, but it just never occurred to her that teachers had real lives outside school. In the restaurant, for example, she was first surprised to see Miss Aldrich with a romantic-looking guy and a bottle of wine, and second surprised that she didn't have her huge, yellow leather briefcase with her.

After history was over, it was noon-time, and Beth ran down to her locker on the first floor to get her lunch and books for her afternoon classes. Sandy was waiting for her, looking very strange — as if she were out of breath, but not breathing very hard.

"Did you hear yet?" she asked Beth.

"Hear what?"

"Old Mr. Maynard died."

"When?"

"Last period."

"Right in class?"

"That's what I'm telling you. I was there."

"Oh, my. Was he murdered?"

"You watch too much TV. He had a heart attack."

"Poor guy. Was it awful?"

"It was mostly fast."

"How did it go?"

"Well, I can't show you here. Somehow that doesn't seem real tasteful."

"You could describe it."

"Well. Well, he was at the blackboard. He was talking about Shakespeare and the types of plays he wrote and he had just written "tragedies" on the board and asked what other kind of play Shakespeare wrote and Bill Wernicke guessed musicals and everyone laughed except Mr. Maynard, which is unusual because he's usually such a good sport. And then he grabbed onto his chest and doubled over. For a minute everyone was just sort of stunned and didn't move, but then a couple of the guys near the front jumped up and grabbed him and propped him up against the desk. It looked like he was trying to say something, but no sounds were coming out. His face was gray. Not like real skin color. And then he just sort of slumped and went completely limp. Someone ran and got Mr. Wendt. He's such an idiot. I mean here is poor old Maynard deader than a doornail, and Wendt is poking around at him like he's got an M.D. and a couple of specialist's degrees. You know, he's looking into his eyes real serious-like and listening for a heartbeat and trying to take a pulse. Finally somebody yelled why didn't he send for a real doctor, which sort of snapped him out of it, and he went off to call the ambulance. You can't believe how quiet a classroom can get until you put a dead body in front of it. Everyone just sat there staring at Maynard, who sat there staring back since his eyes were still open. And I mean this went on a long time. It took maybe fifteen, twenty minutes for the ambulance guys to get there. One of them was real cute."

"What a story," Beth said. "I've got Maynard's class right after lunch. You think they'll have a substitute by then?"

"No. You'll probably just have a study hall."

By the time they got to the cafeteria, there didn't seem to be much more to say about Mr. Maynard. Beth was sorry he was dead, for Mrs. Maynard and their kids and all, but also because he was a nice man, and had steered her on to a few really good poets. He was the kind of teacher who really did care what you were interested in, not just what was in the lesson plan.

Beth found a couple of free seats at the end of a long lunch table and held them while Sandy got her lunch and Beth's Coke. Beth, like most of the kids, brought a sandwich every day. Sandy, who could never get up early enough to fix something for herself, was forced to contend with the mysterious offerings of the Hamilton High cafeteria. Today they were especially mysterious. When Sandy had sat down, Beth looked over her tray. The only recognizable items were the two Cokes. On the large plate was something white and both puffy and slithery. At the moment, it was creeping off the plate on one side like something in a fifties horror movie. Beth stared at it with a mixture of revulsion and fascination.

"What is it?" she finally got up the nerve to ask, still not entirely sure she wanted to find out the answer.

"They told me fish purée. Do you think it's still alive?" Sandy asked.

"What's in the little dish?"

"Mixed vegetables."

"Why are there grapes in it?"

"Well, they don't say mixed with what."

"And the white thing is a boiled potato?"

"It could be a boiled tennis ball. I'll be able to give you a more informed opinion after I've tried to put a fork into it."

"And what's that? Are they trying to pass off stewed prunes as dessert again?"

"Well at least it's straightforward. For a while there, they were doing a prune tapioca. You had to cover it with another plate. You couldn't stand to look at it while you ate. Well, here goes. You know where to find my will."

"Are you going skating tonight?"

"I don't know. Sometimes I wonder if it has any redeeming social value."

"How do you mean?"

"Well, last week, there I was going around and around and around, looking at who was sitting in the stands, and I'd pass all the guys I've known since kindergarten. And I thought to myself, this is what I spent an hour getting fixed up to impress? I mean, really, these are supposed to be the most exciting years of our lives, and for me they're about as stimulating as a nap."

"Do you really buy that? About these being the most exciting years of our lives?"

"No. I mean I'm counting on it not being true, but still, they probably should be a little more exciting than retirement, don't you think?"

"There've been some pretty good parties, don't you think? During the summer and since school started too?"

"Beth. You're talking basements and nacho cheese dip and the whole place smelling like aftershave. Parties — real parties — are when Hype rents a whole villa in Jamaica and Jeremy Dant parachutes in over the bay in front of the house and they go through 400 cases of champagne and have Big Macs flown in from Miami by private plane. The guys in Hype only eat junk food, you know. And all the biggies from the rock world come, and socialites, and in the pictures there are always people in space suits, and ladies with shaved heads, and midgets. And these bashes go on for two or three days. And then everybody flies off to Rome."

"But these are adults," Beth said.

"Not all of them. Some of them are just rock stars."

"But you're not a rock star. You can't play an instrument. You sing like a dying crow."

"But Jeremy Dant is a rock star. Maybe the biggest of them all, and all the articles say he isn't dating anyone in particular, that he's still waiting for the right girl. The thing is, I think, that he's tired of all these fast jet-set types. What he wants is a girl who really loves him, just for himself."

"Someone like you, I'll bet. Someone who's never met him, but is able, through articles in magazines, to divine his inner qualities. Someone who isn't at all interested in the wild life he leads on several continents. Someone who'd be just as mad about him if he settled down here and went to work at Simpson's service station."

"One of your few shortcomings, Beth, is that you don't know anything about spiritual communication and cosmic destinies."

"I just think you oughtn't to go too far off the deep end with this. I mean fantasies about unattainable lovers. Well, I guess everyone has them now and then. But you have to keep your feet on the ground. I mean, I think if you started dating someone from around here, you'd forget about Jeremy Dant in a hurry."

"I can't wait until something like this happens to you. I'll hand you back the same advice and see how much you like it."

"This kind of thing won't happen to me. I'm not being smug. Sometimes I envy you your flights of fantasy. But I know I could never work one up myself. I'm just too practical, I guess."

4

Beth almost didn't go to school on Monday. She had a sore throat and thought that maybe it was a case of rheumatic fever coming on, in which case she definitely shouldn't get out of bed.

On the other hand, it could just be that she needed a drink of water. But to see if that was the problem, she would have to get out of bed, and it was cold this morning, the first cold morning of fall. And her dad hadn't put on the heater yet.

And even if she got brave enough to touch the nice, warm soles of her feet to the cold, bare wood of the floor in her bedroom and the colder tile of the floor in the bathroom, she would still have to go down into the cold kitchen and eat a bowl of cereal with cold milk and go to school and take a chemistry test she hadn't studied for at all.

On the whole, it seemed smarter to just roll over and go back to sleep.

"Did you steal my *Galaxy Heroes* comic books?" was the next thing she heard. It was accompanied by a swat on the head. She turned over onto her back and opened one eye. It was Harry, of course, standing over her.

"What?" she asked.

"My *Galaxy Heroes* comic books. You stole them."

"You're holding them in your hand," she said.

"Dummy. These are my *Space Creeps* comics." He hit her again with them.

"Hey," she said, finally awake. "Cut it out, moron! You think I'd be interested in that drivel you read? 'Space Commander to Space Cadets. Scuttle the reactor!' What I'm telling you is you'd better blast off in a hurry. And if you *ever* wake me up again, especially by beating me about the head with your repulsive comic books, you won't live to see ninth grade."

"I'm really scared. Really. Really scared," he said, hanging around the doorway of her room.

"Arrrrrrgh!!!" she yelled, leaping out of bed and across the room at him. He was gone in a flash. Harry wasn't growing all that fast and at thirteen was still a little smaller that she was. She knew that this blissful situation wouldn't last forever and that she would have to come up with new tactics to scare him when he was no longer afraid she'd beat him up. Maybe by that time he would have done something she could blackmail him with.

At any rate, she was fully awake now and although it was late, there was still time to make it to school if she skipped breakfast. She thought she might as well go. They only allowed so many absences and it was only the middle of October. There would probably be more tests she hadn't studied for than there would be allowable absence days, and she probably ought to ration them out.

The chemistry test was worse than she thought. A big part of it was writing down the chemical symbols for a lot of those later elements that nobody can pronounce, much less remember. She was feeling pretty low about it until she talked with some of the other kids after class, and even the brains said they thought it was an especially tough exam. Maybe she hadn't done all that bad.

By the time she got to lunch, the rumor mill had spread it around that old Mr. Maynard had been replaced by a younger guy who had already assigned a paper in the morning classes. On his first day!

"This is all I need," Beth told Sandy. Another real hard teacher who gives out tons of assignments."

"Besides that, I think he might be a jerk,"

Sandy said. They were in the girls' john. Beth was waiting while Sandy leaned across one of the washbowls to get her face very close to the mirror. She was pulling one of her eyelids very taut so that she could apply a thick black line along its edge. Sandy experimented a lot with makeup and haircuts and styles of clothes, and often surprised Beth by how different a person she could look like from week to week. Today she had on a lot of eye makeup — some of it sparkly and most of it blue. Her hair was reddish blond and very short. She had had almost all of it cut off recently to get rid of a permanent that — on top of her dye job — had turned out strangely. What little she had left looked like the hair on dime store dolls. She was dressed in old jeans and a sweatshirt — just this side of how sloppy the principal's office would let you get before they sent you home to change. Sandy liked to be riding some line of outrageousness all the time. This was just the one she was sitting on today.

Beth wondered how the new teacher seemed like a jerk, so she asked, "How does he seem like a jerk?"

"I don't know. I think he thinks he's hot stuff."

"How?"

"He thinks he's cute."

"That must mean he is cute."

"Not *my* type. He had on a tweed jacket. My Uncle Brad wears tweed jackets. Old guys wear tweed jackets. He probably smokes a pipe."

"I suppose you think he would have stood a lot better chance of getting hired here if he wore leather jeans like Jeremy Dant."

"You won't be defending him when he starts piling on a paper a week."

The paper turned out to be only two pages on your favorite writer and why he or she was your favorite. And Mr. Evans, the new English teacher, turned out to be very cute. Still, Sandy was right about one thing — he was a jerk.

It started off with him taking the roll. ("So I'll get to know who you all are," he said.) The only thing was that he called everybody by last name first. Which was fine for most of the kids, but Beth's last name was Bruce, so it came out Bruce Beth. By the third day, it became apparent that he was going to continue calling everyone by last names, and Beth suddenly found herself a Bruce.

The first couple of times, she didn't even know he was calling on her, and there would be this long silence while everyone waited for her to answer, and she just sat there thinking he had called on some guy named Bruce; and then when she did pick up on it, everyone around her would laugh. Or else she wouldn't pick up on it, and Mr. Evans would repeat, "Bruce, *Elizabeth*" or "*Ms*. Bruce." These first times she didn't think past the awkwardness to casting any blame, but the third time she thought she saw a tiny smile at the corner of his mouth and decided in an instant that he was a jerk.

27

Which was too bad, because he was *very* cute. A very subtle kind of cute. If she had to describe him to someone, it would be hard to make him sound unusual. He didn't have bright blond hair or shiny black — just brown. Neither particularly short nor flamboyantly long. He didn't have a rock jaw or Roman nose or pearly teeth, or any of the stock attributes of the heroes of the romantic novels she read by the dozens.

What he did have were deep, clear, sensitive green eyes, soft-looking lips, a shaving cut just below his left ear, and glasses he looked better without. He took them off between reading passages from books he brought in. When he read, he sat on the corner of his desk and crossed one leg over the other to prop up the book. He had a smooth way of reading aloud. Not like an actor who's just good at repeating lines. More like someone who's so in love with what he's reading that he makes it sound special.

Sometimes, after the silence that always followed, he would say, "I like this, but that doesn't mean you have to. And if you don't, I'm real interested in why not. I don't want to just stand up here listening to my own thoughts."

Which she liked, the way he seemed to care what they thought. Some of her other English teachers had done a lot more telling what books were about than asking what anybody else thought about them.

Then on Friday, he asked her what she thought about a part from *The Great Gatsby*.

"What do you think, Bruce?"

That was the time she thought she saw a smile underneath the serious set of his mouth and the exact moment she began hating him. Over the weekend, she wrote the paper for him and said her favorite author was the guy who wrote *Space Creeps* comics, that she thought the adventures of the Space Creeps were more interesting than anything she had found in books without pictures. She even read one of Harry's issues of *Space Creeps* so she would have something to say about them in the paper, and in case he called her on it.

Which, of course, he did.

When he handed the papers back the next week he dropped hers on her desk ungraded.

"Maybe you could stop by after last period this afternoon," he said.

"Sure," she said, and had an odd thought. She had a lot of odd thoughts where he was concerned. This time, instead of wondering what he was going to say to her, she was thinking it was a good thing she had worn one of her first-string outfits today — light gray corduroy slacks with a light blue V-neck sweater and a navy shirt underneath.

What was going on here? What did she care how she looked for him? It wasn't as if he noticed her. It wasn't even as if she liked him. Actually, he probably wasn't even worth the effort she was putting into not liking him. He was sarcastic and stuck on himself and had told the class one day that Emily Dickinson — Beth's favorite poet — was currently being overrated by the critics. Definitely not a person to care about. Which brought her back to the question of why she did care. Maybe she was going into some new adolescent phase of hormonal imbalance, and this was the first of a whole string of ways in which she was going to start acting screwy. She hoped not. Sixteen had been as tough as she wanted to go through. She was counting on seventeen being a placid lake she could sail across, with college on the other side.

5

She could hardly remember an afternoon creeping by so slowly. Finally, when French was over and the final bell went off, she headed for the girls' john to comb her hair before meeting with Evans. She didn't notice that Matt had come up alongside her until he put his hand on her shoulder.

"Deep in important thoughts?" he asked.

"Oh," she said, surprised to see him. "No. I was just getting a little depressed at all the verbs Mademoiselle Goldberg is making us memorize." It was only half a lie.

"Do you want to go get a Coke with me?"

"I can't. Evans — the new guy — wants to see me. I've got a feeling he didn't like my paper." She told him what she had written.

"I can see where that might get a rise out

of an English teacher. Is he all that bad? The other kids were saying he seemed like he might be all right. Nice guy and all that. Sort of with-it."

"*I* think he's a jerk."

"Then all you can do is avoid him. You can never win, you know. The student never wins."

"I know. From now on, I'm just going to lie low."

"Tell you what," he said, draping his arm over her shoulder as they walked, "I'll wait for you outside his room and we can go for a Coke when you're done."

"Oh, I don't know. You'd better not bother. I think there are other kids he called in too. I'll probably have to wait my turn. And then who knows how long it'll take. I'd feel bad about keeping you waiting. I know. Why don't you head over to Ferguson's and hang out a while, and if I get there in time, I'll meet you. And if I don't make it, just leave without me."

"Okay. I was going to go over there anyway. It'd be great if you could get out of there pretty fast, though. I'd like to take you for a ride this afternoon."

"I'll try," she said, kissing him on the cheek. "This is where I get off," she said when they got to the door of the girls' bathroom.

Sometimes the thoughts she had about Matt surprised her too. Like just now she had — before catching herself — thought what a nice, stabilizing boyfriend Matt would be for Sandy.

When she got to Evans' classroom, he was talking with Sonia Michaelson, a major league gatherer of brownie points. She was probably asking for extra reading assignments. As Beth approached the two of them — they were huddled side by side in two student desks — she could see him writing a list of some kind. Sonia *was* getting extra reading assignments.

He looked up.

"With you in a minute, Bruce," he said. "Have a seat on my desk, why don't you."

She did as he told her, went up to the front of the room and hitched herself up onto his desk. She opened her French book on her lap so she would have something to stare at besides Evans and Sonia. First, she tried to memorize the present tense conjugation of the verb *prendre*. This was futile. Sickening as Sonia's buttering-up was, Beth could not resist eavesdropping on it.

"After I get through the Russians, I want to do the Victorians. I don't feel any of my courses here have covered them nearly well enough," she was saying. "I wonder if you might guide me in that area too."

"Well, why don't we talk about that when you've finished these books?"

"Oh. Of course. I didn't mean I wanted to do anything about it right now. I just wanted you to know how much I appreciate your help. Sometimes it's a little frightening to face all of literature alone."

Beth thought she might throw up if she listened to any more of this. Then, while Sonia cooed on even more, Beth became suddenly distracted. Next to her on the desk was an old, much-handled, hardback copy of the collected poems of Carl Sandburg. It came to her in twin flashes of perception and curiosity that he had probably written his full name inside on the first page, and that she wanted to know what it was.

She edged her right hand out from underneath her French book, while keeping her eyes down as if she were studying the page in front of her. Really, though, beneath the dropped lids, her gaze was slithering right along with her hand as it edged closer and closer to Carl Sandburg. Just as she touched the corner of the cover and began to slowly lift it with her index finger, she heard him say, in a voice that was much, much closer than she thought he was, "It's Terry."

She looked up and saw that Sonia Michaelson was just about out the door and that Evans was standing over her. He was wearing an aftershave that smelled like a mixture of cologne and burning leaves. She was dying of embarrassment. She pretended she didn't know what he was talking about.

"What's Terry?" she asked.

"My name. You were looking for my name. It's Terry."

It would have been easy to deny it, but

for reasons that weren't quite clear to her, she didn't bother. Instead, she looked him straight in the eyes and said, "I thought it was Bill."

"Why?"

"It just seemed like you would be. A Bill, that is."

"Sorry to disappoint you," he said and flipped open the cover of the book himself, "but there it is."

She looked down and saw "Terrence Evans" written in a squat, heavy, stylish handwriting.

"How come you didn't put 'Evans comma Terrence'?"

At first he looked at her like he didn't get it, then like he did.

"Ah. So that's what this is all about," he said, picking her paper off the desk by its stapled corners. He took it, walked halfway down a row of desks, and sat down.

"How about this," he said after thinking a minute. "You do the paper over and I'll get your name in the right order in my head."

"Okay," she said, suddenly shy.

He crushed her paper into a ball, then tossed it over the desks into the wastebasket in the front of the room.

"Good shot," she said.

"You know, I didn't mean to offend you."

"It's okay," she said, now nervous without knowing quite why, but feeling very much that she wanted to be out of there, while at the same time wanting to stay and talk to him for a much longer time. She got up off the desk and then, having done that, but not knowing why, figured she had better follow through and head toward the door.

"From now on, I'll call you Beth."

"Thank you." She couldn't help smiling.

6

Beth's thoughts about Matt being a good possibility for Sandy led her to thinking that at least someone *like* Matt — reliable, good head on his shoulders, clear eye to the future — might be an antidote to Sandy's emotional disequilibrium and overactive fantasy life. She spent most of her time ignoring real, available boys in favor of daydreaming about life among the superstars. Then the rare times she did decide to lower herself and go out with a mere mortal, it was usually some total weirdo. What Sandy needed, Beth was convinced, was some guy who both lived in their town and didn't seem like he just moved there from another planet.

After much thinking along these lines, she came up with Tom Maxon, whose picture was probably next to the word "stability" in the dictionary.

Tom lived on a farm just outside Danube, was big in 4-H, and was planning to be a veterinarian. He was a quiet type, and so wasn't one of the most popular guys in school, but everybody who knew him liked him. In trying to figure out whether or not to fix him up with Sandy, the deciding factors were that he was pretty good-looking (if in a scrawny way that looked a little loose in clothes), that he didn't have a girlfriend at the moment, and that he was one of Matt's best friends.

Matt thought right off that it was a good idea.

"He's too shy. I tell him that all the time. I know he wants to go out more. And someone like Sandy who talks all the time might be just the ticket. She could take up a little of the conversational slack, if you know what I mean."

"Well, don't mention it to him until I've checked with her. I'm going to have to do some paving of the way. She has a natural aversion, as you know, to guys who don't wear eye glitter or set guitars on fire as a hobby."

"Is she still pining away over that bass player? Bo Watson?"

"No. Now she's on to Jeremy Dant."

"Who's he?"

"Lead guitar with Hype."

"Hype? You've got to be kidding. Those

guys look like you could catch something just shaking hands with them. And they're worthless musically."

"Tell *her*. I already know."

"If that's the type she goes for, how're we going to get her to go for Tom? I mean, I don't think he owns a pair of gold jeans."

"That's why I asked you not to mention anything to him just yet. I have to prepare her. I think I can do it, but it'll have to be handled very subtly. But I think when I'm done, she'll say yes."

"N-O," Sandy said when Beth had finished presenting her case. "That is, in case I wasn't being clear enough, capital N, capital O. No."

"By that, do you mean you'll think about it?"

"By that, I mean that if you mention his name one more time in my presence, I'll leave."

"We're at your house," Beth said. "It'd probably make more sense for me to leave."

They were in the kitchen. It was after school. Both of Sandy's parents worked so they had the place to themselves. Beth was sitting at the formica-topped table while Sandy made them a couple of peanut butter and jelly and banana and potato chip sandwiches — the specialty of the house.

"What's wrong with him?" Beth asked. "I won't mention his name, but I think you know who I'm talking about."

"For openers, he has hay growing out of

his ears. He talks to the animals. The only reason he doesn't smoke a corncob pipe is that his parents won't let him yet."

"Ha. Ha. Ha."

"You think I'm kidding."

"I think you're letting the superficiality of your values show."

There was suddenly a burst of scratching and thumping and low moaning and loud barking at the kitchen door.

"MacBeth?" Beth asked Sandy.

"Of course. But do not, under any circumstances, let him in. Dogs have special frequency hearing and can hear, from a mile off, a PB&J&B&PC sandwich being made. He knows there are two of them almost ready in here. We can let him in after we're done. You'll just have to put up with the noise."

"But he sounds so pitiful. I can hardly stand it. Really."

"Beth, if you let that dog in here, he will eat your sandwich in a minute. And when he's done, will he be grateful? He will not. He will just give you a look like you've been an incredible sucker."

"Okay. Why don't we at least go into the living room where we won't be able to hear him so well."

"Sure."

Sandy brought the sandwiches with her and had Beth bring two glasses of milk. Sandy's parents had a stereo system in the living room with a big collection of classical records. Both Sandy and Beth liked rock better, but it made them feel sophisticated to be listening to classical, so they played a lot of those records whenever they were alone, talking. This time Sandy put on something by Tchaikovsky, who was their favorite.

Beth didn't say anything, just ate her sandwich. Nothing she could say would make Sandy give Tom Maxon a try. She had been stupid to think this would work.

After a long while — half of Tchaikovsky's Violin Concerto — Sandy finally said, "You're disappointed."

"Yes."

"In me?"

"No. In myself for thinking I could just run someone else's life according to my own simple-minded plan."

"No. I was the jerk. I'm sorry about the farmer jokes. Maybe he's a nice farmer. One of those deep, serious, independent farmers like the ones Gary Cooper played in the old movies. I just don't think it'll work out. I know I hardly know him, but I just don't think it'd work out."

"I understand."

"Oh, all right. I'll go," Sandy said with a sigh of exasperation at herself and Beth and the whole subject.

"What changed your mind?"

"I don't know. I guess it suddenly occurred to me that he might — if I'm really lucky and play all my cards right — give me a ride on his tractor."

7

The night of the BIG DOUBLE DATE, Beth planned to sleep over at Sandy's afterward so they could talk and play records. She came over at seven with a little canvas sack with her sleep shirt and toothbrush and comb in it. The guys were due at seven-thirty. The plan was to go to the movies, then out for a pizza. Beth and Matt figured that this way Sandy and Tom would have a couple of hours to get used to being around each other without having to talk. Then they could go to Bommarito's and get to know each other better. But if things got a little slow, Beth and Matt would be there to hold up the ends of the conversation.

When Beth got there, Sandy's mom —

whom everyone, including Sandy, called Rita — let her in and sent her upstairs.

"Cleopatra is in the royal bedchamber," Rita said, "balming herself with lotions and potions. She has directed her faithful handmaiden Rita to iron the royal T-shirt. But — pray tell — how does one iron over sequins?"

Rita was like this — a little wonky — a lot of the time. Beth didn't always get what she was talking about, but she always liked her. Sandy liked her a lot some of the time, and not at all others. They had a complicated relationship that involved actually talking about a lot of things with each other, something Beth had a hard time imagining doing with her own mother.

She told Rita not to bother with the T-shirt.

"Sandy's not going to be wearing sequins tonight. She wouldn't happen to have a nice, checked gingham dress, would she?"

"Why? Are you kids going to a hoedown for some square dancing? You could be a swell influence on her, Bethy. Get her into some wholesome activities. Hayrides. Taffy pulls. Apple bobbing."

"Would you settle for a movie and a pizza?"

"Sold," she said. "Here. Take the T-shirt up with you. You two fight it out. We made a deal tonight that if she cooked dinner, I'd iron this. I want to keep up my end of the deal."

"Okay. By the way, did she tell you I'm sleeping over?"

"Yeah. And I'm delighted to have you. I'd like to bid you a fond and warm welcome, and tell you that if you two play the *1812 Overture* at full volume like you did last time, there will probably be a sensational ax murder in next week's *National Enquirer*."

With great effort, Beth talked Sandy out of the sequinned T-shirt and into plain jeans and a clean sweatshirt that didn't have anything disturbing printed on the front. The guys arrived five minutes late, smelling of aftershave and showers and shoe polish. Beth knew it must be Tom's influence. Matt shined his shoes about twice a year.

Tom had brought flowers — an oddly old-fashioned gesture, Beth thought. She was afraid Sandy would think it too corny.

"My mom has a greenhouse," Tom said, as he shyly, clumsily shoved the flowers at Sandy.

"*My* mom probably doesn't even have a vase, but I'll go look," Sandy said. When she was halfway down the hall, she came back. "I forgot to say thanks," she told him.

Beth thought it was getting off to a nice start. And from there, it continued to go pretty well. Actually, she had hardly ever seen Sandy on such good behavior. It was as if Tom, with his almost courtly manners, was setting the pace and she was going along completely.

In the show, for instance, instead of slouching down as far as possible in her seat and throwing her feet up on the back of the seat in front of her until the usher came and told her to move them, she sat nice and upright with her hands folded in her lap, and didn't burp real loud after she drank her Coke.

At Bommarito's, both Sandy and Tom were on the quiet side, although when prodded, both would talk. Sandy asked him questions about 4-H activities. Beth thought she detected a tone underneath the questions — the kind of tone you'd use asking a foreign exchange student about costumes and folk dances in his native land. But Beth didn't think Sandy was being condescending or was even conscious that there was this undertone. And maybe it was just that Beth so seldom heard Sandy speak in anything but a sarcastic tone that anything else sounded funny.

There was a rough spot — a pretty long time while they were waiting for the pizza (cheese, sausage, and green peppers) to come when the guys talked about Hamilton's football team and its chances for winning the district championship this year.

Beth had a mild interest in football, or at least in going to games so she could yell and cheer with her friends and get caught up in the energy the sport generated. But she knew Sandy absolutely loathed it, said she could only think of it as twenty-two dumb guys smashing into each other. She thought pro football was marginally less stupid because the twenty-two guys were getting paid to smash into each other.

The couple of times she had said things like this, Beth had been offended because Matt was on the Hamilton team. Later, she decided Sandy had just been making a jokey generalization, that it wasn't anything to take personally. Not that Sandy thought all that highly of Matt, but she would never say anything against him. She had a code of letting people live their own lives, free from the unasked-for advice and opinions of others.

At the moment, her concern for Sandy was to save her from this football talk, which had been going on for fifteen minutes and didn't seem to have an end in sight. She could tell Sandy was getting close to the limits of her social patience, so she rapidly switched the conversation to the movie they had all just seen.

Unfortunately, it had been one of those Swedish art films. Sometimes strange pictures like this turned up at the Rialto in between the regular American movies they usually played — movies with stars Beth knew and plots she could understand. This one didn't even have anyone in it whose name she could pronounce.

Beth only grabbed at the film as a conversational topic because it was close at hand. As soon as she brought it up, she knew she had made a terrible mistake. Nobody knew what to say about it, and yet — so they wouldn't feel like complete dopes — everyone felt they had to make a stab at some kind of analysis.

Nobody said anything for a while, then Matt jumped in and pulled the tone around to normal.

"But what I want to know," he said, "is why anyone should have to watch this in a movie. I just spent half of this week's allowance to get depressed."

Everyone laughed — Tom included — and things were back on track again.

On track, among the kids at Hamilton, meant keeping things pretty light, at least in public. That is, Beth might talk with Sandy, in private, about stuff that was important or troubling to her. Or she might talk to Matt like that when they were alone (although she did less and less of that lately). But when everybody was together, it was strictly good times.

Beth had a feeling from things Sandy's older sister Tina said, that it was different in college, that friends got together and really talked about the important stuff. And she was looking forward to that. But for now — well, if you pulled that here, at Bommarito's or Ferguson's, the conversation would stop dead, just like it did for poor Tom just now, and someone would say some variation on, "Hey man, don't get *heavy* on us."

When they pulled up in front of Sandy's, Tom and Sandy got out and went up to the front porch.

"Be with you in a second," Matt shouted after them, then turned to kiss Beth.

"We can't get into too much of this matchmaking," he said low into her ear. "It really cuts into my time alone with you."

Sometimes, Beth thought, he could be so sweet it made everything go soft inside her. She leaned in to kiss him. Then, as she closed her eyes, her imagination swept her away and she was kissing Mr. Evans. It was insane. She pulled away abruptly.

"What's the matter?" he asked. "Too much garlic on my breath? You ate the same pizza, so we should cancel each other out."

"I just remembered that Tom and Sandy are out there. It might be awkward for them to have to wait long for us."

Matt squinted through the windshield.

"Looks like that's one worry we can cross off our list," he said.

Beth looked, too, and saw Tom and Sandy by the front door in the midst of a quick, tentative kiss. Beth was amazed and delighted and already patting herself on the back.

"We ought to go professional," she told Matt. "Bethmatt Matchmaking Service."

"We'd better call it Mattbeth. Bethmatt sounds too much like bathmat."

* * *

Half an hour later, Beth was stretched out on the sofa in Sandy's living room.

"What did you think of Tom?" she asked.

"He's very nice."

"Is that all you can say?"

"It's all I can say that'll make you happy. It's all you want to hear."

"No," Beth said. "I want to hear the truth. Whatever it is."

"The truth is that he's very nice. And that I don't want to go out with him again."

"Why? Did something happen? On the porch?"

"No. Nothing like that," Sandy said, curling up in the big armchair across the room, stuffing her bare feet under herself for warmth. It was late and the heat was turned down for the night. Both of them had long robes on over their pajamas — Sandy had her own quilted one and Beth had borrowed an old chenille number from Rita — and so they were snug enough to stay down here talking all night if they wanted. It wouldn't be the first time.

Sandy took a while before continuing.

"As you probably have gathered," she finally said to Beth, "I have no idea what I want. In life. In men. But I do have a few fairly clear ideas of what I *don't* want. And Tom Maxon is something I don't want. He's very nice. And serious. And smart. But he's already moving along ruts he has laid out for himself. Maybe when I'm old and tired of having

49

done it all, I can come back to Danube and check in with him again. But right now I have got to do some living. That boy is going from high school to early retirement — and I'm just not interested in that trip."

"Just because he doesn't have his own jet."

"He doesn't even have his own rowboat. He doesn't need any kind of transportation because he's staying *right* here."

"I don't know what you have against Danube."

"Mostly that it's here. And there's so much not here out there that none of us have seen. So many things we'll never do if we stay here doing all the same things we've already done."

"Did you ever think that what's out there might just be a lot of other Danubes? That people out there are doing basically the same things we are?"

"I'm not expecting to cross the first state line and find green men with horns. But I do think there are differences of style. And I'd like to see a few. I'd like to meet a few guys I haven't known since we were in side-by-side cribs at Sloan Hospital. Does any of this sound outrageous?"

"No. I think some of those thoughts myself sometimes. I don't know that I'd ever have the courage to act on them."

"Beth," Sandy said, suddenly whispering, "I *am* going to."

"Are going to what?"

"Act on my thoughts. I'm going to run away."

"Where? When?"

"Soon. I need more money. A month at most, though. Well, maybe two. It depends if I decide to take the bus or hitchhike."

"Hitchhike. Oh, no. You won't live to see the first state line."

"I've thought of that. That's why I think it'll probably be the Greyhound."

"But where?"

"To Los Angeles, of course."

"Why 'of course'?"

"It's where Jeremy lives."

"Jeremy Dant?"

"You think I'd run away for just any Jeremy?"

"You're running away on the basis of a fantasy about a rock musician?"

"You think I should run away on the basis of a fantasy of becoming a clerk/typist in Toledo? I mean, I might as well start big. And then if Jeremy Dant isn't home when I get there, or we get tired of each other after the first few dates, I can always scale down."

"Oh, Sandy. I don't know about this."

"Beth, I really respect your opinion and all that, but this is my only shot at sanity. I'm going crazy here. Whether you think it's a good idea or not, I've got to give it a try. All there is for you to say is that you promise not to tell a soul, either that I'm planning to go, or where I've gone after I leave."

"I promise," Beth said, because trust required it of her. But even as the words were passing her lips, she regretted them.

Much later that night—four-seventeen A.M. by the lighted dial on the clock next to the bed — Beth woke up suddenly.

She could hear Sandy across the room, breathing the deep breaths of heavy sleep. The sleep of a person smug with big plans and content with a growing bank account. Middle-of-the-night wakings were for those with moral dilemmas hanging over their heads.

What was she going to do? She couldn't let Sandy run off without much money or sense into some crazy rock-world life in California. And if she did go, Beth would hate not being able to tell Rita and Sandy's dad where she had gone. They were sure to be sick with worry. And yet she was bound by honor to secrecy.

Into this tangled switchboard of worries crept a scene. In Mr. Evans' classroom after school, she is telling him the problem and he tells her he will come up with a solution.

8

For a while longer, Beth didn't let herself think about what was going on in her head with Mr. Evans. She just let it happen.

It wasn't that she thought about him all the time, but he did pop up in her mind a lot more often that she expected. Some of the thoughts were about how he looked. Remembering how the afternoon sunlight coming through the blinds on the classroom windows made stripes of gold across his brown hair. Thinking about how nice he looked when he got very serious, and took off his glasses, and rubbed the bridge of his nose.

But a lot of the thoughts were imaginary scenes in which she was asking him questions or telling him intimate details about her life and her thoughts, and he was responding with incredible sensitivity. She always gave him the best lines in these scenarios. It was when she started ending the scenes with them kissing in the corner by his file cabinet that she knew a lot more was going on here than the kind of admiration she had felt last year for Mr. Swenson, who she had thought presented biology in an interesting and easy-to-understand manner.

The worst (or best, depending on which way she looked at them) times were when she was in his class. Fifth period had become the high point of her day. She looked forward to Mondays the way everyone else looked forward to weekends.

Part of this *was* admiration. He *was* a terrific teacher — smart about books, showing how they could mean all sorts of things, sometimes things that hadn't occurred to anyone in the class. And he did this, not in a know-it-all way, but gently, as if he wanted to share his love of books with them, as if his favorite authors were friends he wanted to introduce around.

It was a collegy class. Very informal. There were no assigned seats. He didn't really care if people sat in desks at all. On the floor was okay, or on the window sills. Beth usually sat on the floor, but in the front. That way, she figured, he would notice her, but also think she was serious. She worked hard on seeming serious in front of him. She would die if he knew how easily distracted she was from thinking about Oliver Twist to thinking how sweetly rumpled he looked with his collar unbuttoned and his tie loosened.

By the time he had been at Hamilton three weeks, she was gone on him and knew it. But, for a while after that, she was able to convince herself that all the girls were probably more or less gone on him; she was just a little more on the more side. Sandy had his class in the morning. Beth thought asking her would be a good way to check out the general opinion.

"What do you think of Evans?" she asked at lunch one day.

"He's okay. Not as jerky as I thought at first. He's a little livelier than old Mr. Maynard. He doesn't fall asleep in the middle of his lectures like Maynard used to. His assignments are pretty interesting. And he assigns good books. I guess I'd rate him on the up side of okay."

"But do you think he's attractive?"

"What do you mean?"

"Attractive. As in man."

"He's an old guy."

"He's about twenty-five. Maybe only twenty-four. One time in class, he said that he graduated from college three years ago."

"Twenty-five's too old for me to think about."

"How old's Jeremy Dant?"

"Twenty-three."

Beth didn't even bother responding to this. "Jeremy Dant doesn't smoke a pipe and wear tweed jackets with elbow patches. Believe me, at home Evans wears slippers when he reads at night. And flannel pajamas. And has a cup of warm milk before he tucks himself in. Why are you asking me questions about him anyway?"

"I don't know, just curious, just making small talk."

"Oh, no," Sandy said, giving Beth the fish eye.

"Come on," Beth begged. "Just drop it."

"Oh, no. You've got a crush on him, don't you? Sensible Beth Bruce has a wild crush on her English teacher."

"Would you be quiet. You want everybody to hear?"

"So. It's true."

"It's not a crush. Crushes are for sophomores. I think this might be the real thing."

"When's the wedding?"

"I didn't say he knew about it. I just meant it's real for me."

"Beth, as a friend, I've got to tell you this is a losing proposition. He's never going to notice you. And if he does, then what are you going to do? There must be a school rule against this sort of thing. They'd probably expel you. They'd probably deport him. Really. I think you're better off dropping this while it's still in the blueprint stage. I think it's just one of those things that's doomed from the start."

"I won't be at Hamilton forever, you know. Come June I'll be a graduate and free agent."

"Oh, my. You *have* got it bad. Well, what

can I say? Welcome to the Insane Love Club. I hold meetings on Tuesday afternoons."

Sandy was wrong on one point. Evans did notice Beth. She knew he did. The ways he showed it were subtle, but they were definitely there. Like:

How often, when he was trying to make something clear, he would ask, "Does everyone understand?" and be looking, not at everyone, but directly at her while he said it, waiting for her to nod before he went on.

And how often he called on her to read aloud.

And how once, when she was leaving after the bell, but sort of dragging behind the rest of the class so that she would be the last one out of the room, he looked up as she passed his desk and said, "Nice sweater."

She muttered "thank you" and blushed. And she knew it wasn't just that she thought she was blushing. She knew from the heat in her face and around her ears that she was cooking up a nice, very visible shade of red.

It was probably seeing this embarrassment that made him add, "I wonder if you could tell me where you bought it. I have to get my little sister something for her birthday and that'd be perfect."

"I got it at the Chi Chi Sportique," she said, then got embarrassed all over again, thinking, for the first time, what a stupid name for a store Chi Chi Sportique was. Her embarrassment only got worse when he smiled in obvious amusement.

"It's out at the shopping center," she told him as she practically ran out of the classroom, of course dropping her notebook in the process like a klutz and having to fumble around picking it up before she could get out of there.

In the corridor, she let herself fall back against a wall of lockers, reassembled her books, collected her thoughts, and blew a stray lock of hair off her cheek with a large sigh. If this was what love was like, maybe she'd become a nun. She wondered if you had to be Catholic to do that.

9

"Beth," Evans said as she was leaving class the next day, this time not hanging back to be the last one out. "Could you stay a minute? There's something I'd like to talk to you about."

"Sure," she said, her heart suddenly like a pump in her chest.

Three other kids had stayed behind for one reason or another, and so she went over by the windows to wait. She hitched herself up onto the ledge and sat there. Leaning back, she could feel the cold of the windowpane against her shoulder blades, and the cold from the marble window sill against the backs of her legs. Her calves, though, if she let them dangle straight down, touched the hot radiator. She absent-mindedly started playing a private endurance game, pressing her legs against the radiator for as long as she could, until it got too hot and she had to pull them away.

At the same time, she looked on as he gave papers back to Felicia Hennings and Greg Forman, and gave Felicia a little pep talk about her spelling problems. Then she waited while Brad Reeves shyly lent Evans a record of Carl Sandburg reading his own poems. She had never suspected Brad of having enough sensitivity to own a poetry record. Actually, she had never thought of him in any terms other than a person who smelled bad.

After Brad, there was no one but her. She stayed where she was. Evans started putting books and papers into his briefcase. It looked like he had forgotten she was there, but she knew that was impossible. She would just wait silently until he decided to stop playing games. But then, by mistake, her right foot hit the radiator and the sharp sound of wood heel against metal made him look up with a start.

"Oh, Beth." he said. "I'm afraid I forgot you were there."

"You wanted to see me about something?" she asked, in a tone with as low a temperature as possible.

"Yesterday when you dropped your notebook on the way out, this fell out of it," he said, handing her a piece of paper.

It was one of her poems. Of course, it had to be one of the ones she had been writing about him.

"I guess I could lie and tell you I didn't read it," he said.

She couldn't look at him. Nor could she make a move to leave. It was as if cement had been poured and instantly hardened around her feet. All she could do was stand with her head hanging down, looking at the lined looseleaf sheet on which were revealed the intensity and several of the specifics of her most secret passion. Revealed to the object of this passion. Short of a trapdoor opening beneath her, she couldn't see any way out of what — if she lived to be a hundred — would probably stand as one of the most awkward moments of her life.

"It's not half bad, you know," he said.

"What?" she said, looking up to see if she had heard him right.

"It's really pretty good. I mean, it's not Yeats, but I think it shows promise. And I don't hand out encouragement like this lightly. I couldn't live with the guilt of steering someone into a career that paid as badly as writing poetry if I didn't think that by not doing it, I might be depriving the world of a great talent. My only criticism — I guess I should ask if you want criticism. I mean here I am acting like this is something you handed in."

"No, it's okay," she said.

"Well, it's really just a quibble. I wouldn't give him brown hair. I mean, this is a lush, heightened poem and he's really a hero, like an epic hero. I don't think epic heroes ought to have brown hair. Schoolteachers like me have brown hair. This is the kind of guy who rides a white stallion. I think you've got to give him raven hair or ash or something distinctive."

He smiled after saying this and sat back against the desk behind him. She tried to read behind his expression, but she couldn't. There was no way to know if he knew it was about him and was trying to make her squirm, or if he was so thick that he didn't know and was really just interested in the literary merits of the piece. She decided to push to try to find out.

"But, well, you see, it's almost a real person, and he has brown hair."

"Ah," he said. "I see. I haven't seen anyone in the halls of Hamilton who fits this description and so I thought he was a hero of your own invention. Well, so he's real. Then he's very lucky to have someone feeling all this about him."

"I don't think he knows it. The poems are just for me."

"You say 'poems.' Does that mean you have others?"

"Oh, of course. Lots. I've been writing poems for a long time. It helps me make sense out of things. It's like wrapping up small pieces of my life as presents for myself."

"Would you like to share them with someone else?"

"You want to see them?"

"Very much."

"All of them, or just the good ones?"

"Why don't we say all the ones you want to show off. I mean, you could probably leave out the early ones about your teddy bear and rubber ducky and your 'Ode to Parcheesi.'"

She smiled.

"You should think about doing this, though, about letting me see them. If the poems are very personal, you'll be letting someone else take a look inside you. You may not want your privacy walked in on like that."

"Well, I sure wouldn't want everyone to read them, but you, well I'd like it very much."

"Then I'm flattered," he said. "I'll try to be a good and conscientious critic." He reached in the breast pocket of his jacket, which was not tweed, but camel's hair. He was also wearing a light blue shirt and dark green tie. And jeans. The jackets and shirts changed, and sometimes it was a sweater instead of a jacket, but there were always the jeans and always the tie. It was a slightly off-center combination, neither formal nor casual, and added, as far as she was concerned, to his edge of mystery. Of course, to Beth, nearly everything about him was a mystery.

From his pocket, he pulled a pack of gum.

"Want some?" he asked, holding the pack out toward her, pushing a stick out with his thumb.

"We're not supposed to chew gum in school, Mr. Evans," she said teasingly.

"Oh, my. How could I have forgotten that

important section in the Hamilton Teacher's Guide? Forgive me. I certainly don't want to corrupt any of my students." He said this with a sly grin, and when she tried to reach for the gum, he put it back into his pocket. She made a grab for it as it slid in, and got two of her fingers tangled up with two of his in the process, and in the pocket.

He looked straight at her, did not laugh, and did not pull his fingers away as quickly as she thought he might have. Over the next few days, she had several thoughts about the slowness of his reflexes.

10

Friday night she went ice skating with Sandy and Lorraine Thomas. Matt was in training. All of the guys on the football team were supposed to be in bed by ten o'clock on nights before games. This left Beth and several of the other girls Friday night football widows.

This actually worked out fine for Beth, who loved ice skating, an activity Matt said "would put you to sleep, if you weren't so cold." And so Friday nights, she and Sandy, and most times Lorraine, who was a junior and lived next door to Sandy, went skating together.

In a few weeks, Miller's Pond would probably be frozen over, but now they still had to go to the Cascade, which was worse because it cost to get in, better because it had a snack bar, which was a warm place to hang around and talk to everybody.

Beth was not a terrific skater, but she loved it, loved the click-ssshhhh sound of her blades hitting the ice, loved the speed and grace. Mostly she loved the pure isolation of it. Moving to her own inner rhythms, she felt lifted out of the everyday world, alone and absolutely free.

After they had been skating half an hour or so, Lorraine took a bad fall. Beth saw it happen, but was all the way on the other side of the rink. By the time she got back, Sandy and some of the other kids had got her off the ice and onto a bench.

"Does it hurt?" Beth asked.

"Like a truck ran into it," Lorraine said in a voice tight with pain.

After that, somebody from the rink called the doctor — Dr. Dudley — who was very old and very nice and was the one they called whenever somebody got hurt at the rink. Waiting for Dr. Dudley was the worst part. Beth didn't really know what to talk to Lorraine about. On the one hand, she didn't want to remind her of how much she hurt by talking about her ankle. On the other hand, it was hard to think of a subject besides her ankle that would interest Lorraine at the moment. The best she could come up with was offering Lorraine her hand, which she seemed to appreciate and held on to hard until the doctor came. Sandy opted for the distraction method, talking twenty minutes non-stop about Hype's upcoming national tour, a subject she clearly thought would take anyone's mind off anything else.

Doctor Dudley said Lorraine would have to go to the hospital for X rays, that the ankle could be broken. He called for an ambulance. By now the ankle was looking pretty bad — purple and swollen so much the skin looked shiny.

Beth and Sandy both got to ride in the ambulance, which was pretty neat when they blasted through red lights with the siren wailing. Beth tried to hide how neat she thought it was from Lorraine, who was not in much of a position to enjoy the ride.

One of the ambulance guys was real good-looking, or at least so Beth thought. But then she thought almost all redheads were good-looking.

"He's Jimmy Bradshaw's older brother," Sandy told Beth. "He was one of the ambulance guys who came to get old Mr. Maynard at school. I guess there are five Bradshaw boys and all of them have that same hair. If it's true what they say about red hair and temper, I'd hate to see what the fights are like around their house."

Beth thought about flirting with him when they got to the hospital, but the situation seemed too grave for fooling around. She didn't want to be making eyes at him, distracting him from Lorraine's stretcher and causing him to let go of his end, or tip her off.

At the hospital, he and his partner left on another call as soon as they dropped Lorraine off, so Beth didn't have a chance to pursue the possibility any further. Then some hospital people took Lorraine into the emergency room, leaving Beth and Sandy to wait on a bench in the hallway.

For a while, nothing happened. Then a guy who looked too young to be a doctor came out with a form attached to a clipboard and asked for Lorraine's phone number so they could call her parents.

"Is she going to be all right?" Beth asked him, then realized she was just mouthing what she had heard the concerned friend say in every movie and TV show emergency room scene she had ever watched. As if he were going to say, "No, I'm sorry. I'm afraid the ankle was terminal. Your friend has died."

"Sure," was what he did say. "We're setting it and putting a cast on now. She's going to need a lift home. You too, I guess. We'll call her folks for you. We're real good at that. We have the calming touch." He was a fat guy with a nice smile, and was reassuring. The emergency room was probably a good place for him. Plenty of reassuring to be done here.

After that, there was nothing to do but hang around. Sandy wanted to talk about her escape plans.

"With my experience last summer at the Golden Pagoda, I'll probably at least be able to get a waitress job out in California until I get established."

"Established as what?"

Sandy was silent for a minute. "You know," she finally said, "I guess I never thought things through that far. Until I meet Jeremy, I guess."

"You know, for all your big talk about getting out of the provinces and doing the big, bad world, all you're really talking about it latching on to a guy. Is that your idea of The Goal? Is that all you want — to be somebody's girl, or even wife? What about *you*? What do you want for Sandy?"

Sandy's face took on a slightly stunned expression.

"I don't know," she said, then grew quickly defensive. "Should I?" she asked. "Do I have to have my whole future outlined today? I guess I thought I had a little more time before I had to have all the answers. I didn't know there was going to be a quiz today. I would've studied."

"You don't have to get sarcastic with me," Beth said.

"You didn't have to get preachy with me."

"Touché."

They sat in tense silence for a few minutes. Suddenly, Sandy looked up over Beth's shoulder.

"My, my," she said. "I think I've just found something to get the old conversation going again."

"What are you talking about?"

"Well, if I'm not mistaken, our favorite English teacher is holding a limp body at the check-in desk at this very moment."

Beth turned around. It was true. Evans

and another guy were standing in front of the nurse's desk, propping up between them a girl in a fancy crepe party dress and a full state of unconsciousness.

In a flash, emergency room orderlies came and whisked the girl through the same door that had swallowed Lorraine half an hour ago. The other guy went in with her, and Evans slumped into one of a row of connected aqua plastic chairs out in the waiting room. He put his head in his hands.

"What do you think?" Beth asked Sandy.

"I don't know. But I'm dying to."

"He looks so miserable."

"Why don't you go over and talk to him?" Sandy nudged Beth with her elbow. Beth shrugged her off.

"You just want the dirt. Can't you see he's suffering? What if he doesn't want to be talked to?"

"Well, I think you ought to go over and find out. That is, if you're really concerned about his suffering and not just worried about getting your pride stomped on if he tells you to buzz off."

Beth thought of six possible opening lines on the short walk down the hallway into the waiting room. She had discarded every one of them by the time she got to where Evans was sitting. All she could think of to do was sit next to him.

He apparently felt her presence since he looked up as soon as she sat down. What he gave her was the look of confusion resulting from seeing someone familiar in a totally wrong context. She could tell she did not compute in his head, which was disappointing — she would have preferred him to say, "Oh, Beth, my darling, it's you of all people I need most at this tragic moment in my life" — but understandable, given the circumstances. At any rate, it left her with the awkward task of introducing herself to the guy she was in love with.

"It's me. Beth. Beth Bruce. From your English class."

"I know. I know," he said, although it was clear from his expression that he was just beginning to figure it out. "What are you doing here?"

"A friend of mine broke her ankle skating. We're waiting for it to get set. I saw you come in. You looked sad over here. I thought maybe I could help. Now that I'm here I have no idea how I thought I was going to help. If you want, I'll go away. I won't be offended," she lied.

"No, that's okay. I mean, why don't you stay?"

"You don't have to tell me what's going on," she told him.

He looked a lot different from how he looked in class. In the first place, he was dressed differently — in jeans as usual, but without a tweed jacket or sweater or tie. Just an open pea coat and underneath that a rough cotton shirt in that not quite white color the fashion magazines usually called "natural."

Another difference was that he looked a

new kind of rumpled — not the kind of rumpled he usually was, which Beth always thought of as having to do with staying up late reading, and grading papers, and drinking a lot of instant coffee. This was a rumpled that smelled like sweat, and a little like beer, and seemed to have to do with dancing and having a good time. Only he wasn't having a good time right now.

"I guess maybe I'd better not talk about it," he finally said. "I haven't thought this through real well — not expecting to run into one of my students here — but just off the top of my head, talking about it with you doesn't seem like the smartest thing I could do."

After that he didn't say anything for a while. Then he turned and looked at her hard, as if trying to see inside her. What he finally said was, "Then again, I guess there aren't that many conversational topics available to us here in the old emergency waiting room other than why we're here." He sighed. "Oh, what the heck. She tried to kill herself."

"Who?"

"Her name's Jeanine. She came to the party with Stan. That's Stan who went in there with her. I don't know her. Never met her before tonight. Stan doesn't even know her very well. He's only taken her out a couple of times. I guess she's coming off a bad romance with someone else. She had too much to drink and then shut herself in the john and ate a lot of pills. And then people started to miss her — actually they started to miss the availability of the bath-room. We got the door open and there she was on the floor and someone had to help Stan get her down here and so here I am."

"And so now you're waiting for Stan?"

"No, I could leave. He just lives a couple of blocks from here. He told me he'd just as soon handle it by himself. Actually, before you came up I was just sort of immobilized with depression about the whole thing." He gave a broad, very fake smile. "But now I'm fine. See?"

It wasn't a statement meant to be believed, just accepted, so she went along.

"You need a ride somewhere?" he asked.

"I think I'll leave now."

"Thanks. Sandy and I were waiting for Lorraine's mom. Lorraine's the one with the broken ankle."

"Well, if you don't want to wait, I'd be glad to give you both a lift."

"I'll check with her," Beth said. "Just give me a minute."

When she got back to Sandy, she started talking real low and real fast.

"I don't want to look like I'm telling you his life story so I'll just give you a capsule summary. Some girl at the party he was at tried to do herself in. He wants to give us a ride home, but you want to stay here and make sure Lorraine's mom shows up and that Lorraine's all right, but you also think there's no sense in both of us waiting and since I'm tired, you think I ought to take the ride home he just offered me."

Sandy smiled.

"Thanks so much, Beth. It's been a tiring day and it's such a chore to think and speak for myself. It's nice to have someone do it for me. Have fun. I think you're nuts, but have fun."

"Well, it's not exactly a 'have fun' situation. Even though he didn't know her, he seems sort of shook up. So I don't think he's even thinking about me. But it's a chance to be with him. Alone. And I'm a desperate woman so I'll grab at any straw. I'll call you tomorrow." She squeezed Sandy's shoulder by way of a good-bye.

Out in the hospital parking lot — rudely cold and clear after the stuffy, overheated waiting room — he led her to the oldest, most dilapidated car among the dozen or so there. A teacher's car. Beth wondered if there were special lots where they sold used cars only to teachers — no car newer than ten years old, none without at least one rusted-out fender, all with unbent coathangers for radio antennas.

She went around to the passenger side only to find the door stuck shut with tape. Dozens of strips of heavy-duty black electrical tape.

She looked up over the top of the car to find him looking sheepishly at her.

"I forgot to tell you that side doesn't work. You'll have to slide in over here."

Which she did and then sat there on the cold plastic seat waiting for him to put the key in the ignition and turn on the heater and put the gear shift into reverse and back out of the space. None of which he did. What he did do was sit there, keys in his right hand, resting on his leg, his other hand on the steering wheel, eyes focused vacantly on the middle distance somewhere beyond the edge of the parking lot.

In a flash — a belated flash for sure, but a flash nonetheless — Beth realized that he really was shook up. It made her feel like a jerk, sitting there thinking of this as an opportunity for flirting, blithely ignoring the fact that he was truly upset by the night's events. It was like a fast slap in the face and made her grow up about five years in ten seconds. She tried to think of some way she could help.

"Talk to me," she said softly, not turning or moving toward him. At first she didn't think he was going to, but he finally did, in a low, empty voice, not at all the confident speaking voice he used from the front of the classroom.

"I was just wondering what pushes someone that far. I can't imagine being where she must be. Just the thought of it terrifies me."

What happened next happened very fast, but Beth would remember it clearly for a long time after.

The first thing that happened was that he slumped over very slowly until his forehead was touching the top of the steering wheel.

The second thing that happened was that she reached over and touched his shoulder.

The third thing that happened was that he turned and put his arms around her and pulled her toward him. She felt a shudder go through him. As soon as it passed, he pulled back from her.

He had not hugged her. Not even a far more smitten, lovesick, crush-besotted schoolgirl than Beth could have mistaken what happened as an embrace. He had simply needed someone to be there, to absorb the tremor, and she had been on the other half of the front seat. She was glad she was, but at the same time didn't attach romantic significance to the event.

"Thank you," he said, looking at her with a degree of seriousness she wasn't accustomed to receiving.

"If it's any help," she said, "I think people who jump in front of subway trains are the kind of terrible you're thinking about. I think maybe people who swallow pills at crowded parties where someone's almost bound to discover them in time, are asking for someone to pay attention. Which is sad, but a lesser degree of sad, I think."

"How'd you get so smart at sixteen?"

"Seventeen. You forget I'm an aspiring poet. Suicide seems to be an occupational hazard in my chosen profession. So I've done a little reading on the subject."

"Ah. Well, I'm glad to have somebody around who knows something about this. I sure don't, and it scares me."

He put the key into the ignition and started up the car. "Well, you better give me directions to wherever it is I'm taking you."

"Home," she said and told him the way. It wasn't very far and they filled the time talking about Anne Sexton and Sylvia Plath, two poets who had killed themselves, but it was a school-type discussion, like a conversation she might have with any teacher after class. And then, when they got to her house, he just pulled up in the driveway, slid out to let her out his side since her door didn't work, patted her on the back, and said, "See you Monday. And thanks again."

Like some guy she baby-sat for rather than like some guy she had been out with.

And when she got to his class on Monday, there were no special looks or asking her to stay after for a minute. Not that she really expected there would be anything like that. But still, it confused her a little, almost made her wonder if anything *had* taken place between them.

The more she ran this through her head, the more confused she became. Probably he wasn't giving her any signals because he couldn't. Sure, for one small part of one night, they had been two people sharing an experience. But for five days a week from now until June, they were going to have to be student and teacher. He undoubtedly knew that and was just behaving reasonably.

But then there was always the possibility that he just didn't care, that what happened Friday night had meant nothing to him. Had it all been in her imagination that he had found her especially warm and sympathetic and smart and mature? It was this thought, this possibility, that made her crazy.

And the thing of it was she would never know what was going on with him.

After three days of worrying the problem around and around, she decided she was in a no-win situation and the only thing to do was to pull back from it. So strong was her resolve that she even doubly committed herself to it by telling Sandy at lunch.

"Falling for guys who can't or won't fall back is just dumb. And I refuse to be dumb."

11

The next weekend, Matt's parents were out of town at a wedding, so Saturday night Beth lied to her parents that she and Matt were going to the movies. Actually, he came and picked her up and then drove her straight back to his house.

They had done this a couple of times before when the opportunity had arisen. She could tell Matt thought it was terribly exciting. He talked a lot about what if his parents should suddenly come back.

Boy, would they be shocked if they did, Beth thought sarcastically. What wild goings on they would find. One empty bottle of beer. (Matt would always take one from the back of the the basement refrigerator, figuring a back bottle would be less conspicuously missing. As if his parents did nightly counts on their beer.) Rock and roll music on their stereo. Two teenagers sitting next to each other on the sofa. Sometimes holding hands! If they came in just before Matt was about to take Beth home, they might even see him kissing her once or twice. (Matt was very strict with himself about holding the line at kissing. He told Beth that they had to take responsibility for their futures. And while she agreed with him and was glad that he was this way and not an animal she had to fight off all the time, still, it was one more way in which he was almost too solid.)

This time, to add to the excitement of the beer and the music and the hand-holding, he brought out a can of nuts.

"I think there's a good chance my mom's going to miss these," he said, opening the can with a key that came attached, the pressure escaping with a short, loud sigh. "I don't think she'd miss the peanuts, but these are her cashews."

"Why don't you just tell her you ate them yourself?" Beth asked, getting a little tired of all this fake drama.

"But that's not the kind of thing I'd do, open up a can of cashews just for myself. Eat them all in one sitting."

"Tell her you just went nuts. Ooops. No pun intended."

But he was already laughing. He was easy to get a laugh out of. Sometimes she liked this. It made her feel witty, which she didn't with everybody. Sometimes, though, like now, it just made her feel that he was a little simple.

"Anything special you'd like to hear?" he asked her, looking through the record cases under the stereo table.

"What about some old Stones?"

"Don't you think that'd be a little loud? I was sort of thinking of something a little smoother. To kind of set the mood, if you know what I mean."

Beth thought it sounded as though he had been watching too many of those wine ads on TV. The ones where the couple is in front of a fireplace, always in some place that looks like a ski lodge.

"I don't care. You can put on the Hollywood Strings if you want. That'd either set the mood or make us think we're in an elevator or the dentist's waiting room."

He looked hurt and she felt bad. She hadn't meant him to take the tease seriously.

"Put whatever you want on," she said, trying to go back and recover the same ground. "Then come over here and *you* set the mood for me."

He liked that, she could tell. Liked thinking of this as a hot and heavy romance. She guessed that maybe for him it was.

He put Tchaikovsky's *Pathétique* on the turntable, which surprised her because she didn't remember ever telling him how much she liked the big Tchai. And then he came and bent over the sofa and gave her a quick kiss, which also surprised her, it not being on the usual end-of-the-evening kissing schedule.

"You're a surprising fellow tonight, Matt."

"Is that a compliment?"

"Sure."

"Well then, thank you. But sometimes I think you put too great a value on surprising and spontaneous. Steady is a virtue too, you know."

"Of course," she said, but thought to herself that steady was more something she'd be interested in if she was forty and had three kids and a house half paid for. She tried to imagine Matt at forty. It wasn't too hard. In a lot of ways, he was already forty. Maybe he would weigh a little more and have a little less hair and be more knowledgeable about insurance sales techniques and crab grass removal, but otherwise probably about the same.

It was sort of what Sandy had been saying about Tom Maxon. The difference was that Sandy had an alternative in mind — a dopey alternative, but something nonetheless.

What did Beth have in mind if not Matt or someone like him? Lying up in her room aching with a stupid crush on her English teacher? That was a terrific, mature expenditure of time, for sure.

And she was making fun to herself of Matt for choosing to major in business administration at Siddons. Did she even have a college yet, or a major picked out? Where did she get off being so smugly critical about everyone else's decisions when she hadn't even had the nerve to make any yet?

"Do you want to dance?" Matt asked, still standing over her, still trying, she could tell, in spite of what he had said, still trying to be surprising.

"I don't think you can dance to Tchaikovsky," she said.

"Don't tell that to any of the ballet companies," he said. "They'll never be able to do *Swan Lake* or *Sleeping Beauty* again."

Now she was really impressed. She would have never guessed he knew a thing about ballet. It didn't seem to be a big topic of conversation among the guys on the Hamilton football team. Who knows. Maybe Matt had hidden depths.

"I didn't know you were a balletomane," she said, trying to plumb those depths.

"A what?"

"I didn't know you were a fan of the dance."

"Only by blood. You know Annette's been taking lessons almost since she learned to walk. And because she's my sister, she lives here. And because she lives here she practices here, and so over the years, I've heard more ballet music on this record player than rock."

"Oh."

"But I've never seen anyone try to dance

to it with regular dance-floor dancing. I think we ought to give it a try. If we bomb, we're the only ones who'll ever know."

"Well, put that way, I guess I might as well be a sport."

And so she got up and let him take her in his arms. Matt was so big that dancing with him, there was nothing to do but let him lead. Which was also a pleasure because he was very good. She knew that from dances they had gone to at school. Being an athlete gave him coordination and agility, plus he had a soul that was sensitive to music. It was the perfect combination.

What they did to Tchaikovsky might not have been what the composer had in mind, but it wasn't bad — a sort of free-form waltz, and Beth wished it could go on forever. Holding him lightly as they danced, feeling the soft wool of his sweater under the left hand she had resting on his shoulder, feeling the warm dampness of his cheek against hers, his breath stirring the hair over her ear, she knew that this dance was his way of trying to be more what she wanted. And, because she herself wasn't sure what it was that she wanted, it was a particularly persuasive gesture.

It was times like this — when he filled her with so much feeling that she was sure this must be what they meant when they talked about the Real Thing — that confused her, now that there were so many other times lately when he seemed absolutely, completely, totally, certainly dead wrong.

When Beth got in at midnight, her parents were sitting in the living room, not watching TV or listening to records or reading. It didn't even look like they had been talking to each other. They were just sitting there — her mother in the chair by the window, her dad on the sofa.

"Hi folks," she said, stopping in the hallway, taking off her jacket. "What's up?"

"Us," her father said. Although her mother was in her robe, he was still dressed — in corduroy slacks and a plaid flannel shirt and short suede boots. Her father was a very good-looking guy and a very sharp dresser. Although he had a regular job as manager of a big bookstore out at the mall, he also did modeling occasionally. Stanton's — the big department store in Danube — used him in a lot of their catalogs when they needed what he called "the solid provider look." He told Beth the modeling brought in important money. "It'd be peanut butter casseroles around here without it," he said once.

At the moment, he was slightly less than camera-ready good-looking for he was obviously tired and clearly not wanting to be where he was.

"How was the movie?" he asked her.

"Oh. Pretty good. Nothing terrific."

"Your mother and I decided to go at the last minute."

"Ah."

"We didn't see you there."

"Well, we got there early and we like to sit way up front and then we left while the credits were still rolling, so I guess I'm not too surprised." She didn't lie often, but when she had to, she thought she did a pretty good job of it.

"*We* liked the picture a lot," her mother said.

"Well, good. I mean I didn't think it was terrible or anything."

"Did you like the part about the turtle?" her mother asked. "We especially liked that part."

This was clearly the crucial question of this conversation. If she answered correctly, she was home free and up in bed with two happy parents whose minds had been put at ease. If she blew it, there was heap big trouble ahead.

She thought hard. She should have looked up what was playing before she left the house. Then she remembered passing the show on the way to Matt's. The marquee had said *99 Years in Alcatraz.* She thought and thought and couldn't come up with a likely turtle scene set in Alcatraz, unless they let the prisoners have pets and somehow that didn't seem likely. Nope. This was definitely a trick question, and one she was too smart to fall for.

"What turtle scene?" she asked. "I don't remember any turtle scene."

"How could you forget the whole thing about Bruno's escape attempt? How could you forget anyone snapped to death by a pack of renegade turtles? You kids sure must be innured to violence these days from television, if you could forget a sockeroo scene like that," her dad said.

"I must've been out getting popcorn," she tried feebly, but she knew this was the end of the line.

"You weren't at the show, were you?" he asked.

"No."

"That leaves me — I don't know about you, Alan — but it leaves me curious as all get out as to just where you were if you weren't at the show like you told your trusting, wonderful parents," he mother said, getting up out of the chair and coming toward Beth. "Why don't you take off your coat and stay a while, as they say. Sit on the sofa next to your father. He'll strap the electrodes to your wrists and we can turn the lie detector on."

"Oh, come on," Beth pleaded, embarrassed at having been caught out, now wanting to just get the whole thing over with and take her punishment. "I was at Matt's."

"How do we know you're not lying about that too?" her dad asked. "Maybe I'd better call his parents and make sure they remember you better than you remember the turtle."

"His parents weren't home."

"Ahhh," Beth's mother said, pulling a hard candy out of a dish on the end table next to the sofa where Beth and her father now sat — not at all cozily — side by side. "I can see why we were lied to."

"It's not like you think," Beth said.

"Isn't that Famous Teen-Age Line Number Forty-seven?" her dad asked, looking up at her mom.

"Yes. I think Number Forty-eight is 'All we did was play Monopoly.' "

"Please, you two. I'm sorry I lied. I don't very often. But I knew you wouldn't let me go over there if his parents weren't home, and it's something he likes doing so much."

"I don't doubt it," her father said. "I'm not so old I've completely lost my memories of what constitutes a good time for a red-blooded high school guy."

"Matt's not like that. Really, he isn't. With a lot of the other guys, you'd be right to worry. But being over there for a night is mostly about as dull as being here. Oh. No offense."

"We pride ourselves in providing you with a certain amount of stabilizing dullness. It's what parents are for," her dad said. "But what I'd like to know is why you'd risk losing your allowance for three weeks — that's what's happening to you, by the way — and have to put your coat on and go out into the cold and drive halfway across town, when you can get all the dullness your heart desires right here at home?"

"Daddy, you're asking me the same questions I ask myself. I'd be delighted if you could provide the answer too."

"You don't like Matt?" her mother asked.

"I like him sometimes, in some ways. Not enough, I think. But I think it may be me. I don't like much of anything enough lately. It's probably just The Confusion of Adolescence," she said, referring to a book on one of the shelves in her parents' bedroom. If they teased her about the agonies of being a teenager, she got back by teasing them about all the reading they did to try to cope with her growing up.

"What's the problem, sweetheart?" her father asked, reaching out and pulling her over to his side of the sofa.

"I guess maybe I am a little confused. No big deal."

"I know this is going to sound prosaic, but maybe you're just having senior whim whams, you know, feeling vague about your future."

"Something like that," Beth agreed.

"Why don't you take some action, then, at getting rid of some of the vagueness. Make your college applications so that you get accepted somewhere and know where you're going to be next year. That might dispel some of the driftiness," he said.

"But I don't even know what I want to study."

"That's the beauty of college," her mother said, sitting down on the floor in front of the sofa. "It's set up for you to play around with all sorts of subjects, and ideas, and ways of thinking. Sure, some kids know from the time they're five that they want to be neuro-surgeons, but most people are like you. At seventeen, they don't know enough about anything to know what they want to know about."

"You mean I'm normal?"

"Supernormal," her dad said, tousling her hair in the back. "Sue, how'd a couple of off-beats like us ever get such a normal kid? Where did we go wrong?"

"I'll talk to Mr. Higgins on Monday," Beth said. "He's the guidance counselor. He's got books on all the colleges. I think I'd like to go somewhere small, with incredibly good-looking guys."

They all laughed.

"I'll advance you money for stamps for the applications," her dad said. "Because you really aren't getting any allowance for a while."

"But I *am* sorry I lied."

"I know that," he said. "But you did it, so there has to be some justice. Besides, it'll be therapeutic for me. Otherwise, I'll feel like I've been had, that I was an old crock you thought you could put one over on. I used to lie to my own father and so maybe I should expect that it's my turn to be on the receiving end, but I just can't. I like to think I'm smart and with-it. I haven't had a chance to ask Dr. Stern about this, but I'm sure he'd say it was healthy for me to dock your allowance as a way of saving my pride. You understand, don't you?"

"I never want to stand in the way of mental health," Beth said, smiling in spite of the vision of three weeks' allowance with wings attached to every bill flying out the window.

"Do you want some cocoa?" her mother asked. "I have a taste for it."

"Thanks, anyway," Beth said, "but I think I'll just go up to bed. I'm real sleepy."

"Well, don't worry so much," her mother said. "About the future or about Matt either. There are going to be lots more. The next one you'll probably like too much and he won't know you exist. You've got so many wonderful problems to look forward to."

Once she got into her nightgown and between the sheets, Beth was suddenly not sleepy at all. While she had been talking with her parents, they'd made it all seem so easy. Now that she was alone with just her own thoughts, everything seemed complicated again. And as she got sleepier, thoughts of Mr. Evans started creeping in. How could they, after she had so convincingly talked herself out of him?

As she was just about to go to sleep, a real person came creeping into her bedroom. She opened her eyes to see Harry standing in the doorway.

"I just wanted you to know," he said, "That if you're ever in financial need, I'd be glad to help out." He must have been listening to her and her parents from the stairway.

She could hardly believe her ears.

"Hey, Harry, that's really sweet of you."

"We can discuss my interest rates tomorrow. I charge by the day."

"You have a truly sick mind," she told him turning over to face the wall and end the conversation.

12

Tuesday night, Beth was at the supermarket, doing some shopping for her mother. She was working overtime at being superdaughter. She felt bad about having lied to them and wanted to make up for it as much as she could.

She looked down at the list her mother had written out:

lettuce
whole wheat bread
window cleaner
milk
brownie mix

The first three items were fakes, or at least stuff her mother could get along without until she went shopping herself tomorrow or the next day. The real reason for this trip was the last item. Beth's mother was a chocolatoholic and tonight she had a heavy brownie craving. The milk was a legitimate item too. She liked to have it to drink with her brownies.

Another reason Beth didn't mind running this errand for her mother — aside from assuaging her guilt — was that it gave her the car and a chance to get out of the house and away from studying for a little while.

She thought she might drop by Matt's — just for a couple of minutes. After school, she had put a protein beauty pack on her hair, then blown it dry, and it looked really terrific. Actually, according to her bedroom mirror just before she left the house, *she* looked pretty terrific tonight. She had on her favorite pair of jeans — too old to wear to school anymore, but perfect-fitting and, after three years of wearing and washing, faded to a perfect dusty blue. On top she was wearing a bright green sweater and her navy, down-filled vest. And for the *pièce de resistance*, her brick-colored leather boots, the Christmas present she had begged for last year and polished so often since that they looked even better than when she had gotten them.

What a waste — looking this good and no one within miles to impress. She thought more about driving by Matt's. He probably wouldn't notice the specifics, but he usually picked up on the general effect. At the very least, he would be surprised and probably pleased at her just dropping in unannounced on a week night.

She had already been in the check-out line for ten minutes when she realized that she had forgotten the window cleaner. To go back for it meant losing her place in line, and ordinarily she would have just told her mother she had forgotten. But she was really aiming to please lately and not look like a goof-off to her folks, so she went back to the aisle that had cleaning supplies.

And who was there, standing right in front of floor waxes, but Mr. Evans and a truly gorgeous blond, about twenty, and obviously really tight with him. The two of them were almost out of control with laughter, probably at some in-joke. Beth's first impulse was to try to slink away unseen, but of course she would have this rickety old shopping cart with front wheels that refused to obey, and so turning around in the narrow space of the aisle took forever and produced so much wheel-squeaking that Evans and the blond were forced to look up and see what all the commotion was about.

"Hey!" Evans called when he saw her. "Hey, Beth!"

There was no slinking off now. It would look stupid. She straightened the cart out and wheeled her way up to them.

"Hi there, Mr. Evans," she said and nodded a vague hello to the girlfriend.

"Doing some shopping?" he asked. It was such an incredibly stupid thing to say. If Matt had said it, she would have given up on him as terminally banal. And so she knew it was a sure sign of how far gone she was that she found it charming that Evans could say something so dopey and awkward, just like everybody else. It made him seem so much more human somehow, and therefore so much more possible for her.

"Yeah. My mom's a chocolate freak. I'm getting her a brownie fix," she said, nodding her head toward the box of mix in the cart. "Of course, after I make them for her, I'll probably have a couple myself. Her passion is playing havoc with my figure."

"Oh, I don't think you have to worry," he said. "You seem to be about the right weight for your height and bone structure. Oh, I'm sorry. I forgot my manners. Beth, this is my sister Casey."

Beth couldn't believe the relief that flushed through her as she said "Hi" to this person who was instantly removed from the category of competition.

"Beth is the student I was telling you about," he said to his sister. "The one I get my fashion tips from. If it weren't for her good taste, you'd probably have a sweater with a deer head on it. As you can see," he spread his hand out in Beth's direction, "I only go with the best sources. Girls who look terrific even on late-night trips to supermarkets."

Later that night, in bed, Beth thought about how she could have said, "Well, I figure it pays to be prepared in case any big Hollywood talent agents have started hanging out here at the Mighty Mart." But at the time, her head was too full of blood from blushing to allow for the formation of snappy come-backs.

"Terry tells me he really likes teaching at Hamilton," Casey said. "Are you one of these bright students he's been telling me about?"

Beth laughed. "No. I think I'm probably one of the lazy students he hasn't been telling you about."

"That's the only kind there was when I went there."

"I *thought* I recognized you."

"I graduated two years ago. Maybe you remember me from football games. I was heavily into cheerleading when I was at Hamilton. That's about all I *was* heavily into."

"And now you go to college?"

"Yeah. Westerly."

"What're you into up there?"

"Well, they don't offer a major in Pom Pom, and so I got into psychology."

"Do you think a wax that says it's for linoleum would be okay for wood floors too?" Evans asked no one in particular. He had apparently left the conversation for the moment and was surveying the selection of products to make floors shiny.

"N-O!" Casey told him, taking the can out of his hand, putting it back on the shelf and taking another one with a wood pattern printed right on the can.

"I'm home for a couple of days while our mother's in the hospital," Casey told Beth. "Tonight we're cleaning her house for her."

"Nothing serious?"

"No. She'll be home tomorrow and in bed another week or so, they say."

"Do you need a ride?" Evans asked her as he and Casey headed up toward the checkout counter.

"No. Thanks. I've got the car."

He got a few feet away before she said, "I'll try to bring those poems in sometime this week."

He turned and looked at her blankly, but just for a second, and then said,

"Oh. Of course. Sure. I'd be glad to look them over. Anytime."

And then he was gone and Beth stood in the aisle wondering if it were possible that he had forgotten. It seemed he was always one step ahead of her being able to figure him out. He had definitely noticed how sharp she was looking tonight, but then what kind of remark was that about her weight? It was the kind of thing she expected to hear from old Doc Snively, her old pediatrician. And then his getting absorbed in looking over the fascinating wax selection while she was talking with Casey didn't seem to show an overwhelming interest in her conversation.

Did he like her? Was she anything special to him? Was there any possibility of that happening? Or was he just a compulsive flirt? Or an unconscious one? Or was he just behaving no way in particular while she was laying her own interpretations on everything, so that what looked to her like something was really nothing at all?

She puzzled through this set of thoughts all the way home. By the time she got there, walking through the door that led from the garage into the kitchen, she realized that she had forgotten both the window cleaner and the plan to stop at Matt's.

Her mother was in the kitchen waiting, reading a magazine at the table in the dinette alcove.

"I got the double fudge kind," Beth told her, as she unpacked the grocery bag. "Do you think they'll be too chocolaty?" Beth teased.

"Stop torturing me and let's get this show on the road. I already put out the bowl and eggs. Do you want me to help?"

"No. That's okay. With the mix, they're easy. Just stay and talk with me while I mix them up."

"You got some phone calls while you were gone."

"Sandy and Matt."

"How'd you ever guess?"

"I'll call them back when I get these in the oven."

"So," her mother said, lighting a cigarette, exhaling smoke dramatically, as if they were two characters in a play, about to start an important conversation. "What's new with you?"

"I ran into my English teacher at the Mighty Mart."

"Did you talk to her?"

"Him. A little. He's sort of nice."

"Is this the young one? The replacement?"

"Mmmmhmm," Beth said, her arm already tired from beating the heavy brownie batter.

"How young?"

"I don't know — twenty-four, twenty-five."

"Do you have a crush on him?"

Beth was shocked. Did it show? Was she wearing a sign on her back?

"Why would I have a crush on him?"

"I don't know. I had one on my English teacher."

"How'd it turn out?"

"He had nine kids. I used to dream about him and me, and then he asked me to baby-sit for him once. After that I could only think of us falling in love and his wife leaving and me getting charge of the nine kids. It cooled me off considerably."

"This one isn't even married."

"Well, it's still a losing proposition. I mean if you were thinking about getting stuck on him, head yourself off at the pass."

"Why?"

"Well, high school teachers and their students are not generally well-received couples in our social set. So, if he falls in love with you, you've got trouble. If he doesn't, you've got misery. That's a hundred percent chance for unhappiness. A literal example of something there's no percentage in."

Beth wasn't used to talking like this with her mother. Mostly, they kept things on the surface; they didn't get into deep stuff with each other. A big part of this was how her mother was — detached and distanced. Not just from Beth, but from everybody. She was smart and funny and nice and kind, but you got the feeling where she really was was a private place somewhere inside her and no one — not Harry, not even, Beth suspected, her dad — ever seemed to really be able to find that place. She had a job as a loan officer at the Hastings Bank and Beth knew she wasn't crazy about it. She had majored in drama in college, and Beth thought she probably felt frustrated at never having been able to really do anything with that. But this was just a guess. Her mother never came out and said anything like that.

Maybe this signaled a small change — a closer relationship between them. It would be terrific, Beth thought, if they could have a lot of conversations like this in which Beth wouldn't have to give away any of her secrets, but could get smart advice anyway. Maybe after a while she would even start feeling like letting her mother in on her deeper thoughts.

On this issue, she knew her mother was dead right — that Evans was a losing proposition. She licked some brownie batter off the wooden spoon she had used to beat it with and felt a new wave of anti-crush resolve flow through her.

She put the pan of brownies in the oven, checked the time on the clock, and turned back to her mother, who was stubbing out her cigarette in the ashtray.

"I wish you could quit smoking," she told her mother.

"You and me both, kiddo," she said, but didn't sound too hopeful.

She went downstairs and used the phone in the laundry room — as she always did because it was more private than the one in the front hall — and called Sandy. They only talked for five minutes because Sandy was only allowed five-minute phone calls. This was Beth's fault and went back to a major fracas Sandy had gotten into with her parents last year. She and Beth had been on the phone for an hour and a half one night. It was when Beth was breaking up with Bob and needed someone to go over all eight hundred ramifications of the situation with. Which would have been okay if Sandy's dad hadn't come in from a business trip that night and found his car smashed into in the airport parking lot and been trying for fifty-eight minutes of the hour and a half to get through to Rita to come out and get him. By the time he got home — by means of an exorbitantly priced cab ride — he had had plenty of time to work up a rage at Sandy that had carried through to this day every time he saw her with a receiver in her hand.

And so now they crammed all the important stuff into five minutes every night and held the rest over for lunch the following day. If there was something that couldn't hold, they only lived four blocks from each other and one or the other could scoot over.

Tonight, Sandy wasn't much interested in a big conversation anyway. Beth caught her as she was in the middle of memorizing the major human bones for biology, which she had flunked the year before for not memorizing stuff like the major human bones. If she didn't pass this time, she wouldn't graduate.

"Do you know which one's the tarsus and which is the metatarsus?" Beth teased her.

"I'm not going to be a bone surgeon. I just have to pass this test. All we have to know is that they're both in the foot."

After she hung up, she got up and got a Coke out of the basement refrigerator, came back, stretched out across the tops of the matching washer/dryer combo — her favorite place for serious phone conversation — and looked at her watch. Still twenty minutes to go on the brownies, plenty of time for a call to good old Matt. Ten minutes more than she needed as it turned out.

The first five minutes were taken up with him sounding very strange and far off before he got to the point. Which was eventually got to by her asking him if he wanted her to get tickets for the rock concert Saturday night. The bookstore that Beth's dad ran was also a ticket outlet. If they got tickets through him, they would be a couple of dollars cheaper.

"Well, the thing is, Beth . . ."

Well, the thing was that Matt didn't think

103

they ought to go to the concert because he didn't think they ought to date anymore.

"I don't mean not ever," he said. "Just not so steady as we have been. What I mean is I think we ought to give ourselves a chance to see more of other people."

"Matt. Stop. Are you breaking up with me?"

"I wouldn't put it that strongly."

"I don't care how strongly you'd put it. I want to know if you're breaking up with me."

"Okay. I'm breaking up with you. I just don't think it's working out all that well. And there are some other people I'm interested in spending more time with."

"Your parents."

"Come on."

"*You* come on. These other people you keep mentioning — what's her name?"

"It's Freda Toth."

"Freda Toth? Oh, please tell me you're joking. Please tell me I'm not being thrown over for someone who always has food in her braces."

"They're not braces, she only wears a retainer now and I've never seen any food in it."

"It must be love if you make a distinction between braces and a retainer."

"This conversation is degenerating."

He was right, of course, and she was the one pulling it down to a low level. She was sorry she had let herself do it.

"Well, I guess there's not much more to say," she said. "I'm really not mad or anything." She was furious. "The only thing is how disappointed I am in you for doing this on the phone. It's such a chicken's way out. It's really the only thing that disappoints me."

The thing that really disappointed her, of course, was that he had broken up with her before she had had a chance to break up with him. And for Freda Toth! The double indignity of it.

It took her until after two A.M. to get to sleep. She went from angry to sad to lonely to trying to figure out a way to convince her friends that she had subtly pushed him to the point of breaking up with her in order to save his pride. Then she worried for a few minutes that this was not a terribly mature thing to do. She got to sleep by letting herself off the hook. She could start being mature when she turned eighteen.

13

When she woke up the next morning, it was with a start. And with the sudden, sickening realization that she was without a boyfriend. And without anyone at Hamilton (at least among the student population) who she was even interested in making a play for.

She envisioned a bleak future of dateless Saturday nights. She could probably become a much better skater. Get closer to her family. Catch up on all the back issues of *National Geographic* she had up in her room from the subscriptions her grandmother had been giving her for the past five Christmases. She could take up a hobby. Join her church youth group. Somehow none of these possibilities excited her enough to get her out of bed.

Harry — Mr. Sixth Sense for Bad News — came in and sat on the edge of her bed.

"I was accidentally on the extension last night when you called Matt."

"You little nit. Harry, why are you so rotten to me?"

"Why? I don't know. I guess I never thought it through. I guess we've just sort of worked into a comfortable arrangement."

"This may surprise you, but did you know there are actually brothers and sisters who *like* each other?"

"Somehow that just doesn't seem like our style."

"I guess not," Beth said. "Now, will you get out of here? For disliking me as much as you do, you sure spend an awful lot of time hanging around here."

Her mother called up the stairs twice for Beth to get up before she finally did. She would have to skip breakfast.

In the shower, standing there spacing, letting the hard streaks of hot water beat down on her shoulders, it dawned on her that almost none of the funk she was in had to do with Matt. She was feeling bad because she was now without a standing date, without someone to show up with at parties, without someone whose picture she could tape to her dresser mirror. She didn't miss Matt, she missed having a boyfriend.

Poor guy, she thought. How little she must have cared about him if she couldn't really work it up to miss him the day after he had dumped her.

And so she was surprised that she cared enough to be made furious and nauseated at the same time — that time being the moment she spotted him and Freda Toth holding hands and looking dippily at each other by his locker that morning before classes. Well, he sure didn't waste any time, she had to say that for him.

Sandy was unruffled by the news, as she was by most news that didn't directly concern her or Jeremy Dant. Beth told her the whole story at lunch, while they shared Beth's tuna salad sandwich. The cafeteria was serving kidneys that day.

"I didn't think you could serve parts like this in this country," Sandy said, looking morosely down at her plate.

Beth folded her lunch bag flat and laid it over the kidneys, as if they were an accident victim.

"We'll be able to eat better if we don't have to look at them," she said. "Matt broke up with me last night."

"You're kidding?"

"Nope."

"Well, it's a good thing he did. You probably would've never got around to breaking up with him. That deal was — if you don't mind me saying so — a real time-bider. Now that you're free, you can get on with the real stuff."

"Like joining the Future Nurses club? Or taking up weaving?"

"No, dope. Like taking up Evans. I've been rethinking the possibilities on that one, and I figure why not?"

"You're crazy to even suggest that."

"Of course I'm crazy. That's why you'd better listen to me. You've got too much sanity going on around you, you're going to suffocate in it. Now's the time to listen to your crazy friend and put a little insanity in your life."

"I just went to a lot of trouble to talk myself out of this. I'm not going to listen to this," said Beth, who was very much listening.

That night, Beth went through all her poems. A lot of the old ones didn't seem very good to her now. Some were embarrassing and she threw these out. Most of the good ones were more recent and she picked eleven of these. She had wanted to give him a neat ten, but all eleven were so good she just couldn't narrow it down any more.

Six of the poems were about him, two obviously so.

It was a bit of a gamble, she knew. Giving him the poems would lay it on the line. After he read them, he would know. He would be forced to acknowledge her feelings and either accept or reject them. If he rejected her, she knew she would be devastated. She would have no more refuge in dopey hopes and fantasies and illusions.

All of this scared her, but she was convinced it was the only way. She had flimmed and flammed, wished and washed too long. Every time she had told herself this was foolish, she had believed it less. She was plainly in love with him and, at seventeen, had a right to be. The only thing that made this a silly schoolgirl crush was keeping it secret from him.

The other thing she was convinced of was that the way she felt had nothing to do with Sandy's advice, which she never took anyway. Or with the break-up with Matt, who she had never really loved anyway. Or with her mother's warning, which she thought eminently sensible coming from a mother, and certainly nothing she wanted to rebel against.

What she felt for Terry Evans was simply what she felt for Terry Evans, and she knew now that she had to give it her best shot, then accept whatever results came.

Putting it this way to herself, matter-of-factly, it all seemed so reasonable that a great calm descended upon her. She put the poems in a folder — no scented envelope or colored ribbons. She was presenting her love straight.

Then she went down to the basement, switched the radio on and from her mother's classical to her rock station — there were times when Tchaikovsky wouldn't do, when it really was a matter of roll over Beethoven — put the volume up, and ironed half a dozen shirts for school, doing little bursts of boogie while she stood at the board.

When she was done, she went up to her dad's office and typed letters requesting application forms from the four colleges Mr. Higgins had recommended when she saw him this afternoon — two in Ohio, one in the East, and one in California.

Then she went up to her room and took a test in one of her mother's magazines. The test was called "How To Do You Right" and showed what clothes, and hairstyles, and colors of eyeshadow were right for you. She filled in that she was five-six and one hundred and fifteen pounds, and had medium-length brown hair and blue eyes and fair complexion (she wasn't sure about this, but the other choices like ruddy or olive sounded even less like her), and put "average" or "medium" for a lot of other answers and could only think of one problem area — her hands, which she thought were too large for her body. And she found out that she should use blue shadow and wear an easy-care hairstyle and highlight her cheeks with blusher and wear youthful clothes and not wear large, gaudy rings.

Full of all this self-awareness and the inner peace of having a plan of action, she went immediately and soundly to sleep.

She gave Evans the folder of poems the next day after class, then waited for him to make the next move. It took a week.

"I read your *oeuvre*," he told her during class, as he was passing back some corrected papers. She had expected him to find a more private moment. She also made a note to look up *oeuvre*.

"And?" she asked after class.

"Well, let's see," he said, pulling a thin appointment book from the inside breast pocket of his jacket. "Tomorrow's Friday already and I have appointments. Next week is Thanksgiving and that sort of crowds things up. What about the Monday after that? If you buy me a cup of coffee, I'll give you my critique in the glorious Globe Snack Shop, where we can have a little literary privacy."

As usual, she walked away confused. If he had read the poems and got their message, why was he putting her off a week? And if he had somehow been so thick as to not see himself in them, why did he feel it necessary to discuss them in private?

Whatever was going on, she had no choice but to wait until a week from Monday to find out what it was. Over the Thanksgiving holiday, she ate way too much leftover turkey and cold mincemeat pie with whipped cream out of a nervousness that had replaced the one night of blissful calm she had had. She also wrote a really good poem about being confused in love.

On Heavy Monday, she showed up at Evans' classroom after school a deliberate ten minutes late. He was in his jacket — a pile-lined, nylon, dark green jacket she hadn't seen him in before and thought he looked especially good in. He was sitting cross-legged on top of his desk in the front of the room, bent over a book, lost in it.

She waited in the doorway until he felt her presence and looked up.

"Milton," he said, lifting the book.

"Do you like him?"

"Not too much. I admire him a lot, though."

"What's my oeuvre? I tried to look it up but I couldn't find it."

"It's French for 'work.' It means your body of work. Your poems."

"Oh."

"Are you ready?" he asked.

"Yes."

"Then it's off to the glorious Globe," he said, hopping off the desk, and ushering her out the door by touching her shoulder, then quickly removing his hand once they were in the hall.

On the way over to the Globe — a two-block walk — he was real chatty, on light topics. Did she think Hamilton was going all the way to the play-offs? If she was so good with style in clothes, did she know anything about interior decorating? What color sofa should he buy for his apartment? The walls were white and the rug navy.

The Globe was a decrepit luncheonette with flecked formica tabletops and chairs and booths in a bright blue vinyl, old and patched with black electric tape in many places — not the place she would have chosen for her romantic rendezvous. Hardly anyone was there when they came in — four o'clock, the dead valley between lunch and dinner. There was one old lady making a meal out of a cup of coffee — loading it with half a dozen paper packets of sugar and what was left of the cream in the tin pouring container. And a workman — big and beefy and red-faced — having a hot turkey sandwich with gravy and mashed potatoes and soft white bread rolls.

Evans guided her to a booth along the side wall, near the back. She took this as a sign that he didn't want the conversation overheard.

"Coffee?" he asked her as they were getting out of their coats.

"Tea."

He signaled for the waitress and ordered for them both. Then he pulled her folder from his briefcase. He had written "Bruce" on the outside with a felt tip marker, as if he had to distinguish it from all the other folders of poems he was looking over.

Maybe he was. Maybe she was just one of a dozen, or even two dozen students he was interested in helping.

Well, if she hadn't been anything special to him before, the poems had at least singled her out in his mind. She was now, if nothing else, the girl who had made a fool of herself over him — baring her deepest feelings on 8½ x 11, lined looseleaf sheets. In ballpoint ink.

He opened the folder and pulled out the poems, then looked through them as if to refamiliarize himself with them. When he was done, he took off his glasses, closed his eyes, and squeezed the bridge of his nose, rubbing the red indentation where his glasses hit. Of his small repertoire of gestures, this was her favorite.

He was still doing it, still not looking at her, when he said, "Well, you know, some of these — as I'm sure you're aware, seeing as they're the ones you chose to show me . . ."

Here it comes, Beth thought.

". . . are really quite good. Rough in spots, but promising."

"What do you mean — rough?" she asked.

"Well, unpolished. I think you're using your innate sense of word play, but not stretching to impose shape on them." He had put his glasses down on the table and stopped rubbing the bridge of his nose, but he still wasn't meeting her gaze. He stared for a long moment at the top poem. Reading upside down, she could see it was one of the hotter ones.

"This one, for example," he said, lifting it slightly, but then not saying anything more.

She couldn't tell whether he was concentrating hard, forming his thoughts, or whether he was embarrassed.

Then the waitress came with his coffee

and her tea. He seemed grateful for the interruption, and dragged out putting in his sugar and cream into almost an event. When he was finally done, and had taken a couple of sips of coffee, he looked straight at her for the first time.

She wished she could read his mind. In class, he had a look — not smug, but very self-possessed. No one walking into the room would have to ask who was in charge, even if Evans was slouched in one of the back desks, as he sometimes was when one of the kids was holding the class. But now he had completely lost that look of confidence. It was becoming clear to her that he was terribly uncomfortable with the situation, getting more so by the minute, and running out of ways to stall.

The more nervous he got, the calmer she became. She could sense that she was getting control of the situation, and it made her a little giddy. It wasn't a turn of events she had expected. She thought, why not push it a little? Just for fun.

"What do you think," she asked, in a tone rosy pink with innocence. "What do you think of my choice of subject matter?"

"Well, I liked this one about spring," he said, pulling a sheet out from near the bottom of the stack. "The way you bring in the notion that the season has sounds as well as the sights and smells everyone usually connects with spring."

"What about the romantic ones?"

"Are they all about the same guy?" he asked. "The one with the boring brown hair?"

"Yes," she said, suddenly shy.

"You really ought to ask him. He's really the intended audience for these poems."

She almost said, "Well, I am asking him now." But her courage dropped out from underneath her. She was ninety-nine percent sure he knew he was the subject of the poems. And what he was probably doing now was challenging her to admit it.

She just couldn't do it.

"Maybe I will sometime," was what she finally did say. "Not just now, though."

"Why not? Do you think it's one of those admiration from afar set-ups, and if you start dealing with him as a real person, it will all crumble? That sometimes happens, you know. You can build up a lot of illusions about someone that way. No one has pimples if you stand far enough away."

"No. It's not that. He would be very good up close too."

"How do you know if you've never *been* up close?"

"I look for signs. He's got all the good ones."

"Then what's stopping you?"

Things had shifted again. Now he had the edge. Was he using it to tease her? Or was he trying to find out more about how she felt about him? Or (remote possibility, she thought) was he still laboring under the misapprehension that they were discussing a third party?

"I don't think my chances are very good," she said.

"I don't either."

She was startled. It wasn't what she had expected to hear.

"Why not?" she asked.

"Because if you feel as strongly about him as the poems indicate, he probably knows. And if he hasn't responded by now, he probably won't."

"Because he's not interested?"

"There are lots of possible reasons besides not interested. Oh. Sorry."

Their hands had accidentally brushed against each other as they had both been reaching, without looking, for packets of sugar.

He looked at her hard.

"You have an amazing way of looking very here and very far away at the same time. I've noticed it in class several times. And you're doing it now."

"I guess I am both where I am and far away at the same time, lots of the time," she said.

"Right now, I guess I'd like you to be only here."

She could see he was sorry he had said it almost as the words were passing his lips. He brought his voice back fast, from intimate-across-the-table to classroom crisp.

"Well, if we're going to get you started on

the road to obscurity and poverty as a poet, we'd better get to it. I hope you don't mind, but I took the liberty of marking these up in red pencil to show you where I think you could come up with harder images, or better rhythms."

And from there on, for the next half hour until they left, it was all business, followed by a brisk farewell.

"Let me know if I can be of help in the future," he said to her as they parted in front of the restaurant. He sounded like someone who had just finished installing her storm windows.

She stood and watched him get into his car and drive off in the same direction as her house. He hadn't offered her a ride.

Maybe she should run off to California with Sandy, she thought. She sure didn't understand men or boys around here.

14

That was the way Beth thought of Sandy's plan to run off to California — as sort of a joke. Something to tease her about. And talk about half-seriously.

And if Beth ever got a little nervous that it would happen, she could always push back the worry with the certainty that if Sandy ever did start moving closer to taking action, she would talk about it for weeks in advance, giving Beth plenty of time to talk her out of it.

And so Beth was stunned when, just after eleven A.M. of the Sunday two weeks after Thanksgiving, the phone rang and she answered to find a near-hysterical Sandy's mother on the other end of the line.

Sandy was gone.

"Do you know anything about this?" Rita asked Beth in an odd mother-tone, rather than her usual Rita-tone.

Beth ducked, figuring she had better first find out how much Rita knew.

"Did she leave a note?"

"Yes. It says, 'Am off to seek fame and fortune. Will write if I find them. Will be back if I don't. Please don't worry about me.' So what's this all about?"

"Beats me. She never said anything about going anywhere."

Beth hated lying to anyone, but especially to Rita, whom she liked a lot. And especially about something so important. But it was a question of honor over honesty. She had promised Sandy never to reveal anything about her plan, and now she was stuck with that commitment.

"Well, can you think of where she might've gone? I mean, did she ever talk about any places she'd like to see someday that she might've suddenly decided she had to see today?"

"I can't really think of anything."

Beth began desperately wanting the conversation to be over. Anything she could say would have to be a lie, at least by omission.

"Do you really think she'll be all right?" Rita asked. Beth could tell by the crack in her voice that she was beginning to cry.

"Hey. I *know* she's all right. She's probably a real capable traveler. Didn't she just go somewhere last year?"

"That was only to Chicago to see a play with the young people's group from our church. There were fifteen kids and ten adult counselors. I mean, she probably had to find the bathroom in the theater by herself, but we're not talking Magellan or Marco Polo here."

"Well, if anybody could learn to do well on her own, it's Sandy. I mean, she's not going to take candy from strangers, if that's the kind of thing you're worried about."

"You're probably right, but we've called the police anyway and reported her as a missing person."

"Good idea."

"I thought you thought she wasn't in any trouble."

"I don't. And I don't think she's likely to get into any. I just think she'd be better off practicing being capable right here in Danube. You know, for a long time, I've thought of Danube as a set of training wheels on real life."

"Beth. I haven't got the time right now to stop being worried and start being insulted, but I just want to mention that Danube *is* real life for me."

"Oh. Sorry."

"S'okay. I'll have to hang up now. I want to call some of her other friends. Maybe she said something to somebody. Do try and think back if she mentioned anything."

"I really can't remember anything. But I'll call if I do. And please let me know if you get any word. I'm not worried, you understand, just interested."

Beth hung up and went into the kitchen. She had just had a big Sunday morning breakfast with the family, but she needed some food for thought, a heavy-duty thinking sandwich. She could never work through complicated problems without something to chew on at the same time. And there was nothing better to chew on than a sandwich.

Actually, it was Sandy who had opened Beth up to the wide world of sandwich possibilities.

"A sandwich," she had said once, "is as many kinds of anything you want between two slices of anything else. People will try to keep you in line with ham and cheese or egg salad, but they have narrow minds. They won't allow themselves to see the logic and beauty of a blueberry pie sandwich on rye."

Beth thought about this and other good things Sandy had said, as she made a sandwich that was a real tribute to her — leftover baked beans, Swiss cheese, Thousand Island dressing, and avocado slices on whole wheat.

She took this and a Coke up to her room and sat down with it on the floor, her back propped against her bed. When she finished eating, she got out the only Hype album she had — a present from Sandy, of course — and put it on her portable record player.

She and Sandy had never agreed on Hype. Beth thought they were a mediocre band.

Sandy ranked them in the all-time pantheon of rock along with the Beatles and the Stones. She said you had to see them live to really understand their magic. Sandy had gone to St. Louis to catch them once when they were on a national tour. For three days after she got back, she walked around in a fog of ecstasy. Lorraine, who had gone with her (Beth didn't have the money and wouldn't have wanted to blow it on Hype if she had), told Beth it probably wasn't ecstasy, but loss of hearing. She said what Hype mostly was was loud. Her ears had rung the whole bus ride back, she said. She also said they had a lot of neat effects with light and smoke all over the stage.

Minus the smoke and lights, piped through the small, tinny speakers of Beth's record player, they didn't generate much excitement. But she listened anyway, because it was Sandy's music, and might help her think about Sandy in constructive ways.

The third cut on the record was "Headin' West," and featured Jeremy Dant singing the lead. It had been one of their biggest hits. She listened to him sing:

> I'm leavin' Aline, girl
> 'Cause it's all that I've seen, girl
> And I'm not lookin' back
> Just headin' West.

It wasn't until this refrain had played three times that the large imaginary mallet came thudding down on her head, causing her to see — all in one, giant, gift-wrapped package — the solution.

Sandy wasn't in California. She was in Aline, Iowa — birthplace of the one and only Jeremy Dant. Stopping off there — "to get a better idea of where Jeremy's coming from" — had always been a part of the plan. Beth had just forgotten about it. Ever since Rita's call, Beth had placed Sandy irretrievably lost in huge, far-away California. But she was just in Aline, which wasn't far and was so tiny she was bound to find Sandy there. Once she found her, she could probably talk her into coming back.

She got up and ran down to the laundry room and called the bus station. It rang forever. It always rang forever at the bus station. Finally, an extremely bored female voice answered. Beth asked how much a ticket to Aline was and when the next bus for there left.

"Just a minute."

After ten minutes, according to the wall clock over the washer, she came back on.

"Two hundred forty-two dollars and eighty-seven cents and it leaves Tuesday morning from Chicago. There are lots of buses to Chicago. Do you want to know all of them?"

"Two hundred forty-two dollars? Are you kidding? For a trip to Iowa?"

"Iowa? Oh. I thought you meant Aline, Alaska. Iowa. Just a minute."

Only eight minutes this time.

"Two o'clock this afternoon. You get into

Aline at four-eleven, and it's twenty-three sixty-five round trip."

"That's more like it. Thank you."

Twenty three sixty-five was probably extremely reasonable. However, it was about twenty dollars more that Beth had in liquid assets, in cold cash, at the moment.

She thought for a minute, then bounded up the stairs. Her father was in the living room, reading the Sunday paper.

"Beth. Are you practicing for the track team, or just trying to drive me nuts?"

"Sorry," she said and climbed real softly up the stairs to Harry's room.

His door was closed. She knocked.

"*Entrez.*" Harry had taken to using his vocabulary of twelve French words lately.

He was lying on his bed with his shirt off under the sun lamp his dermatologist had prescribed. He had little pads of cotton batting on his eyes and, under the light, looked absolutely and ghoulishly white. He couldn't see who had come in.

"Identify yourself," he said.

"Your favorite sister. I've got a business proposition for you."

"You are in need of financial assistance. Am I correct?"

"Yes."

"And you are curious about the low-interest family rate at HB Finance."

"I guess."

"How much do you need?"

"How much've you got?"

"A couple hundred dollars."

"Two hundred dollars! How'd you ever get that much money?"

"I save my allowance."

"You must've been saving since before you were born. I need twenty-five, better make that thirty-five, of it. Right now."

"HB likes to know the reason for loans it makes. Is this a home improvement loan? A vacation loan?"

"Come on, Harry. Charge me your usurous rates. Just give me the money."

"If you tell, I won't charge you any interest."

"I'd rather pay than tell."

"I'd rather not give if you won't tell," he said, switching the lamp off, removing the pads from his eyes, sitting up, and smiling at her.

"You'll tell Mom and Dad."

"I won't. I'm beyond that."

"Beyond nastiness?"

"No. Just beyond that particular kind of nastiness. Really. You can trust me. You have to trust me. There's no place else you're going to get thirty-five dollars immediately and on the sly, which I gather is what you need and how you need it."

And so she told him. What she had to do and why she had to do it.

"I'm disappointed."

"Why? What'd you think I was going to tell you?"

"I don't know. But something juicier than

this. This is noble and boring." He gave her fifty dollars from an envelope in the back of his top desk drawer. "In case you run into any extra problems. I hope you get her back. I'd hate to see anyone waste all that bus fare on Jeremy Dant. I could play better guitar than he does, with my feet."

"Thanks for the extra. I'll try to get it all back to you as soon as I can."

"No big hurry. *I'm* not planning to run off to California. When are you going?"

"The bus leaves at two."

"What are you going to tell Mom and Dad?"

"I don't know."

Which was the truth at noon. By one o'clock, she had run through seven possible lies and come around to the amazing and highly original idea of telling them the truth. Mostly, she was sick of all the trouble lies were causing her lately.

And then her parents came up with the amazing and highly original response of saying it was okay if she went. They both agreed it was the only way to get out of her moral predicament, and probably the best shot at getting Sandy to come back home. Her dad even offered to drive her to Aline.

"Thanks," Beth told him, "but I think if I just arrive by myself on the bus it'll be less intimidating to her. I mean, I don't want to drive up like the Highway Patrol."

By one-thirty, she was at the bus station buying her ticket. Her dad had brought her over. The girl in line behind them asked him for his autograph. He blushed just like Beth did when she was embarassed.

"I just model sports jackets," he told her. "I don't star in movies."

But she insisted, and he finally scrawled his name across the top of the bus schedule she was holding.

At the ticket window, they found out the last bus out of Aline was at eight at night.

"I'm trusting you to be on that bus, baby," her dad told Beth. "Sandy or no Sandy."

"Okay."

"I haven't had a lot of time to think this through," he admitted. "But it seems safe enough. I mean, you can't think of anything dangerous that could happen to you on the bus?"

"No. Nuns ride them all the time, so they must be all right."

"How soon does it leave?"

"Half an hour or so. You don't have to wait with me."

"Of course I'll wait with you."

"Isn't there a football game on?"

"It's not important."

"Not at all?"

"A little."

"Go. I brought a book. I'd really rather read than talk to a football-demented person."

He kissed her on the cheek and was gone.

It was only fifteen minutes or so before her bus was announced over the public address system. It was a little ridiculous to have a public address system. The waiting room of the Danube bus station was about twice the size of the living room in Beth's house. The girl behind the ticket window (who was probably also the girl who answered the phone; she seemed to be the only employee there) could have stuck her head out the window and called out the buses just as effectively. Beth guessed the recorded public address announcements were to give the place an atmosphere of having entered the modern age.

There were five other people getting on the bus, which was stopping at about a dozen towns before Aline. The driver was standing by the open door of the bus, taking everyone's tickets as they got on. Beth thought he looked awfully familiar, but then decided it was just that he was so cute she wished he were someone she knew. She gave him her ticket.

"We have a snack stop when we get to Grand Valley," he told her as he pulled the top copy off her ticket and gave her back the two bottom carbons. She hadn't heard him mention this to any of the other passengers.

She got on the bus, walked toward the back down the narrow aisle, and found an empty pair of seats on the left. She took the one next to the window. She watched as they pulled out of Danube, and then onto the superhighway for maybe twenty minutes, then off at the Tuckerville exit, then past all the grain elevators and machinery stores and then past the shopping center, then through the residential section with its old frame houses with wide front porches and on into the small downtown with its shoe store and bank and insurance agency just past which the bus pulled to a stop in front of a luncheonette that doubled as the Tuckerville bus depot. She watched this process repeat itself half a dozen times as the bus lumbered in and out of Dewey, Excelsior, Hapsburg, and three or four other towns before this milk run special finally pulled into the big (by comparison) bus station in Grand Valley. By the time it did, her curiosity about the cute bus driver was exceedingly piqued.

He turned around in his seat as the other passengers filed off past him. He wasn't paying attention. He was smiling at Beth. This flustered her a bit — someone she didn't know looking at her so directly.

When she got to the front of the bus, he took off his bus driver cap, exposing a head full of bright red hair. It was then that she recognized him. He was Jimmy Bradshaw's brother, the ambulance driver who had taken old Mr. Maynard away and brought Lorraine to the hospital when she had hurt her ankle.

Apparently he could see the flash of recognition across her face.

"I wondered when you were finally going to get a handle on me," he said.

"I guess you look a lot different in gray

than in white. Plus the cap. It hides your most distinguishing feature."

"Yeah. I like the whites better. And this uniform carries too much responsibility."

"What do you mean? With the ambulance you had to save dying people."

"Yeah, but while I'm wearing this outfit, I'm strictly forbidden to kiss cute girl passengers."

It wasn't something Matt or any of the guys she had dated would have said. This one was bold.

"You're very bold," she told him.

"Well, I've got this one twenty-minute stop to make enough of an impression on you to get you to go out with me sometime. I can't afford to waste a lot of time."

"You could waste the first ten minutes, don't you think? I mean, I don't think you have to be selling yourself the whole time."

"I guess you're right. How about that cup of coffee then?"

"Okay."

"Are *you* going to be sorry."

"I thought you said I was going to be crazy about you by the time we got back on the bus."

"About me, sure. How could you resist? But about the coffee — it's the worst north of the Mason-Dixon line. It's rumored to be filtered through an old sweat sock."

"Old but clean?"

"Don't ask questions you might not want

answered," he said, but smiling, so she knew he was just putting her on.

He turned out to be right on both counts. He was terrific and the coffee was undrinkable. He was very funny, and a fast talker.

She asked him if it was the driving he liked, if that was the connection between his last and current jobs.

"Actually, I'm a philosopher, but the pay's so lousy in my field, I have to do this on the side."

"I know what you mean. I'm an aspiring poet."

"You're definitely going to need a job. You might like driving too. Truck driving maybe. Lots of girls getting into that now. It'll give you arm muscles. Yours look a little underdeveloped to me. You better give me your phone number."

He ran his sentences together so fast that at first she thought maybe her phone number had to do with her arm muscles.

"Huh?" she said.

"I'm going to have to go and start taking tickets in a minute and I don't want to forget to get your number. I'd like to call you sometime." She must have been looking stunned or something because he went on in a real slow, overpronounced voice — "I'd like to ask you for a date. You know, a date. It's a great American institution. We see a movie, then we go get a Coke and you tell me what college you're going to next year and how you're going to miss your dog while you're gone. And I tell you how I'm really an earnest fellow. Saving his money for law school."

"Is that true?"

"Yes. But I don't spread it around too much. Makes me sound dull."

"I'm used to dull," she said, thinking of Matt.

"Then you are ready for a change of pace. Me." He laughed and then spun off his stool. "Got to get those tickets from all our happy passengers. You don't have to rush, though. Bus doesn't leave for ten more minutes. They pay you if you order a second cup of coffee."

And then he was off, putting his cap back on, stopping just as he was about to push open the coffee shop door, and turning toward her as he tipped it, then going out.

When she got on the bus again, he winked at her but didn't say anything. An hour later, they pulled into Aline. She was the only passenger to get off there. He opened the automatic door and called after her as she descended the steps, "My fortune-teller says you should expect a call from a red-headed stranger."

She turned around and voiced the question that had suddenly struck her.

"What's his name?"

"Rick," he said. "What's hers?"

"Beth," she said as he nodded and closed

the door and pulled the bus out onto the main street of Aline and away.

She looked around her. Well, at least there weren't a lot of places Sandy could be hiding. Aline was what, in Westerns, they always referred to as a one-horse town. Actually, it was so out of the way and left-behind-by-time looking that it might still be a one-horse town. At any rate, there wasn't a car in sight.

What there was was a feed store. And a bar — the Toy Tap. And the building that the bus had left her standing in front of. A gas station. Well, there were two gas pumps in front, but the building was also apparently a general store, and there was a neon COFFEE DONUTS sign in the window.

She didn't think Sandy would have had any reason to go into the feed store, or enough nerve to go into the Toy Tap, so this seemed like the obvious place to start tracking her down.

No one was inside. Beth went over to the small lunch counter and sat down on a stool to wait. She looked around. It was a truly amazing place. Probably a person could get just about anything they wanted in here. There was food — canned food and boxed food and a case of frozen food and a meat counter and a dairy case. And clothes. There was a rack of dresses and several shelves of jeans and workshirts. And shoes and boots against the back wall. And shaving cream and toothpaste in another area. And a magazine rack and a turning rack of paperback books. And high up on top shelves radios and even two small portable TVs. She started thinking of things she could ask for just to see if they had them tucked away somewhere. But then, if they did, she would have to pay for them, and she didn't want to blow any more of her travel loan than she had to.

After maybe fifteen minutes of sitting in what was dead silence but for the steady hum of the pop cooler at the end of the counter, someone finally came out from a curtained doorway at the back of the store. A middle-aged woman with very black, very dull hair — as if someone had rubbed it with a piece of coal — done up in an elaborate mass of curls on top of her head. It was hair that looked like it should be sitting on top of a head connected to a body wearing a floor-length evening gown. It was a pretty amazing match with the lank cotton housedress and old cardigan sweater the woman was wearing.

She came toward Beth. Which got Beth thinking how she should start asking about Sandy. As it turned out, a lot of detective work wasn't necessary.

"Well, I see we got another one," was what the woman said. Beth turned around to see who the woman could be speaking to, but there was no one else in the place.

"Pardon?" was all she could come up with by way of response.

"Well, we seem to be getting a run of visiting little girls today. 'Nother one came in this morning."

"She's my friend. I'm looking for her. Do you know where she went?"

"Doesn't take much to know everything that goes on in this town. Population's only forty-five. Even with a big load of visitors like today, that only kicks the total up to forty-seven. Your friend went over to look at the Dant place. I know she didn't visit with them 'cause they're at a wedding in Hooperton this weekend. Still, she found enough interesting about the place to stay half an hour. That's how long it was before she was back here. I guess she was ready to go then. Trouble is, the only bus out of here going west leaves at ten-fifteen every night."

"And so?"

"Well, we played canasta for a while. Then she had a grilled cheese sandwich, an order fries, and a strawberry sundae, and then I let her read through the magazine selection. Right now, she's taking a nap on the cot in the back."

"I see."

"You want me to go get her for you?"

"No, that's okay. I can wait. The only bus out of here going east doesn't leave until eight o'clock."

"Eight-eleven."

"I guess you'd know."

"You play canasta?"

"No."

"Gin rummy?"

"A little."

"Why don't you just stay right there then while I get a deck. Are you hungry?"

"Yes."

"I can fix you a sandwich before we get started."

"How about a cheeseburger?" Beth said.

"How about a grilled cheese?" the woman countered.

By the time Sandy woke up and came bleary-eyed and slightly confused out into the store, it was after six o'clock and Lana (that was her name) had trounced Beth in twelve straight games of gin.

Sandy was not nearly as surprised to see Beth as Beth had suspected she would be.

"I sort of thought you might put two and two together and come up with four fast enough to catch me," she said, sliding onto the stool next to Beth. "But all you've done is wasted a nice Sunday. I'm not going back."

Beth expected this reaction and was prepared to do some heavy selling on the joys of Danube and the wisdom of restraint. But it was rough going. For one thing, there was Lana to contend with — aiding and abetting Sandy from the other side.

"A woman's got to follow her heart," was Lana's position, which she expressed at several junctures in the conversation. That this method of directional determination had led Lana into four marriages and false career starts in seventeen states, and at forty-seven years old, had left her all alone, making grilled cheese sandwiches and selling shaving cream in Aline, Iowa, seemed to Beth a heavy argument against Sandy's flight plan.

But Sandy remained intractable. As she explained it to Beth, she had thought out all the options, knew this was probably not the most reasonable decision, but it was *her* decision, the first real big decision she had made on her own, and she was sticking by it. And, of course, Lana was there to back her up.

"Atta girl," she said, slapping the back of Sandy's hand in a show of camaraderie.

It was then that Beth saw the possibility that Lana was, if not directly influencing Sandy, at least generating an atmosphere that would surely make it hard for Sandy to back down on her decision, if that was anywhere in her mind.

"Lana," Beth said. "Are there any tourist attractions around here? As long as I'm not going to get Sandy back, I guess I ought to salvage something out of the trip — see the sights or something."

"Boy, I don't know," Lana said slowly, thinking hard. "I guess Sawmill Creek is about the only place around here that anyone would want to see. It's sort of pretty out there. Everyone goes swimming there in the summer and skating in the winter. It's probably pretty deserted now. And it's getting dark. You probably won't be able to see much in this light."

"That's okay," Beth said, grabbing Sandy's arm with one hand and both their coats off the glass-fronted, white metal meat counter, over which they had been thrown. "How far is it?"

"Oh, 'bout a mile, I guess. Go to the left when you get out of here, then fork off at the giant topping can."

"The giant topping can?" Beth and Sandy said, not exactly in harmony, but close.

"Yeah, it's a huge whipped cream can. Maybe forty feet tall. There used to be a plant here, but it went out of business. The can's still there, though. It's really the only monument we've got here in Aline. And if we take it down, it'd be impossible to tell anyone where to fork off for the creek."

Beth and Sandy walked a long way without either of them saying anything. Beth didn't want to squelch things by putting on too much pressure. Maybe just being around would influence Sandy somehow.

Eventually, Sandy broke the silence.

"You think I'm being a dope."

"No, I think you're half being a dope and half grabbing for a kind of freedom that looks good to me too."

"What's the dopey part?" Sandy asked. Beth knew it was her cue; she sensed immediately that Sandy was a person wanting to be talked out of something.

"Doing it this way. Upsetting Rita and your dad. Going before you have enough money. Quitting school when you're only a few months from getting your diploma. Just to go after a superstar who — because he *is* a superstar — is probably a class-A jerk. I mean, guys who have entourages of fifty and fans numbering in the millions are hardly ever humble, deferring, gentle souls."

140

Beth thought she might have blown it there, criticizing Jeremy Dant, but she hadn't been able to control herself. Sandy didn't say anything for a while, then said:

"There was a basketball hoop on the front of his parents' garage."

"So?"

"So before he was Jeremy Dant — heart-throb to America's rock and roll lovers — he was just shooting baskets in the driveway like every other guy I know. I mean, for this I'm giving up life as I know it?"

By then they had arrived at Aline's only monument. They both cracked up, doubled over, and laughed so hard they had to hold on to each other. When she could just barely get her breath, Sandy said, "You know, I wouldn't have believed it, but there are some places that actually make Danube look good."

Beth knew then that the dam of Sandy's will had cracked. From there, it was easy to talk her out of the ten-fifteen bus going west and onto the eight-eleven bus going east, which, this particular night, pulled in and then out of Aline at eight-thirty-six and eight-thirty-seven, respectively.

On the way back, they talked for a while; sang, softly, some of the songs they liked best; and then fell silent watching the darkness pass outside the window, punctuated by the lights of an occasional gas station or radio tower.

"You know," Sandy said, "after graduation, I'm really going to go away. Someplace good."

"You won't have me coming after you on that one. You might have me coming with you, though," Beth said.

"You? I thought you were all tied up with a heavy future. What about college?"

"No one has accepted me yet."

"What about Evans?"

"Are you referring to Terry Evans, Teacher of English, Man of Mystery? I told you about our little session at the snack shop. I have no idea what he's thinking." She sighed. "What can I tell you, Sandy? He makes me crazy."

Sandy laughed.

"What's so funny? My life is a laughing matter?"

"No," Sandy said. "I was just thinking how much I love love. Even when it's not mine. Even when it's making my best friend miserable."

"Well, this one isn't going to make me miserable much longer. I'm going to arrange a showdown with that slippery character."

15

The following Tuesday, which was also the Tuesday of the last week of school before Christmas vacation, Beth came home from school to find two letters in the mailbox from two of the colleges she had applied to.

She stalled as long as she could — changed into grubbies, old jeans, and a sweatshirt; got a Coke from the refrigerator; went up to her room; put a favorite record on; put the letters side by side on her bed. By then she could stand the suspense no longer. She tore open the letter from Spears, which had been her first choice. It was a rejection. Sorry, but . . . etc.

She thought of waiting until her mother got home from work and asking her to open the second one, but that seemed like a chicken's way out. It was from Barton, which had been her third choice out of four. It was a small college in Pennsylvania, progressive, with a creative writing program that was supposed to be good. The reason it wasn't her first choice was that it wasn't prestigious like Spears, or close to home like the University of Illinois (her second choice, which she hadn't heard from yet).

Somehow, these objections vanished in a puff when she opened the letter and found it was an acceptance. Suddenly, Barton seemed like the neatest possible place anyone could spend four years. She would have put on her Barton sweatshirt and run up and down the street in jubilation. But she didn't have a Barton sweatshirt so she contented herself with calling Sandy. Who wasn't home.

And so she walked over to Ferguson's, which took her half an hour. There were only three or four kids there whom she knew, none of them her close friends. But she told them anyway, and had a couple more Cokes so she could wait around and see if anyone else was going to come by.

Matt did. With Freda Toth. They had their arms around each other. Not just when they came into Ferguson's, but the whole time they stood next to the booth where Beth was sitting. This whole time wasn't all that long. She asked how they both were, a question she was not all that interested in the answer to. It actually alarmed her a bit how little jealousy she could work up about him. All she could think of was that she knew all the jokes Freda was having to listen to now. She even had a vision of Matt and Freda in their middle age, sitting in front of the TV set, and during a commercial Matt was telling her one of his terrible jokes, or talking about a new life insurance plan he was trying to sell someone, and she thought to herself, "Beth, my girl, you are well out of this one." Which might have just been a defense mechanism, but she doubted it.

Still, she didn't care so little about him that she didn't want to impress him a little. She told him the news of her acceptance.

"Barton?" he said bemused. "Isn't that one of those schools that advertises on matchbook covers, where you can get training by mail in air-conditioner repair?"

"Ha. Ha. Ha," Beth said. Actually. It was a pretty good joke for Matt. For a moment she had an awful feeling that he was getting smarter and funnier just as she had lost him.

"No, really," he said. "That's terrific. I haven't heard of it, but if it's one of the places you wanted to go to, that's what counts. Four years is a long time. Freda's going to come to Siddons with me," he said, giving her a squeeze, which Freda responded to by nodding and giving a smug little smile. Like a Squeezy Smiley Noddy Doll, Beth thought.

There was a little more chit chat before Matt and Freda moved on to a romantic back booth. Enough time for Beth to see that Freda was wearing a signet ring almost identical to the one Matt had given her. She still wore the ring occasionally. It didn't hold all that

145

much sentimental value for her and she liked it for itself. But now she knew she could never put it on again. She didn't want to look like she was a member of some club of Matt's Women.

Lorraine came in a few minutes later and was properly impressed with Beth's news.

"Wow! That's terrific! And that means I'll have a real close friend in college. Can I come and visit?"

"Of course."

"I think my folks would really let me do that too. If it was to visit you. Maybe I'll even be out of this by then," she said, not having to point. It was so clear she meant her ankle, which was still in a cast and, according to the doctor, would be for several more weeks, a fact that had had Lorraine dragged for quite a while.

"You seem more up than usual," Beth told her. "Are you just getting used to it or what?"

"No. Not really. I was getting to the point where I could accept not being able to skate for a while, but now I'm depressed again on account of the Christmas Ball. I was really looking forward to it. And I think, I'm really almost positive, that Joey Flynn would have asked me to it too. But who's going to ask someone with a satin pump on one foot and a ten-pound plaster bootie on the other?"

"Well, at least you can take heart in the fact that someone would have asked you. I've got two good feet and no date."

"Is that true?"

"Yeah."

"Gee, I just assumed you were going. Or I would have asked you earlier."

Beth knew right away that "Asked me what?" was a question she didn't want the answer to, but she couldn't see any polite way out of asking it.

"Asked me what?"

"Well, since I couldn't go and everyone knew I couldn't go, they hooked me into heading up the refreshment committee. And I'm in desperate need of someone to help me manage the cookie and punch table."

"Ah," Beth said.

"Come on. It's only for three hours. And you'll get to see what everybody wears. And we can talk. It won't be bad. And there's really no shame for you not having a date for the dance. Everyone knows you and Matt just broke up."

"Okay, okay," Beth said.

Actually, she didn't mind all that much. A year ago, the Christmas Ball would have been one of the major things on her mind this time of year. But now, with her head having been so full of breaking up with Matt, and rescuing Sandy from a Lana-life, and wrestling with all the emotional complications Evans was giving her, and thinking about her future, she had actually forgotten about the dance.

Another sign of how her perspective had changed in a year was that she could remember going to last year's Christmas Ball with Bob and feeling a shiver go through her as they came into the gym. She might even have said something as dippy as, "It really does look like a winter wonderland." Actually, she was sure she had said that. She just liked to cloud over memories of her worst lines.

This year, when she came in, admittedly an hour before the dance started, and with Lorraine, and carrying a large plastic punch bowl, the gym looked decidedly like the gym, only buried under an avalanche of glittered cotton batting and aerosol snow, with tinsel draped from the basketball hoops. Was it possible that, in one year, she had crossed the line from romantic to cynic? Or was it just that the lights were still up?

An hour later, standing behind the punch table with Lorraine, watching the dancing couples whirl by under swirling colored lights, she had to admit the place looked better, but she still felt compelled to comment to Lorraine, "You know, no matter what they do to this place to gussy it up, it still primarily smells like sweat."

Evans was one of several teachers serving as chaperones for the dance. Beth was interested to see that he hadn't brought a date. Beyond that, she wasn't allowing herself to waste her curiosity on him.

Yesterday, the last day of classes before Christmas, he had announced to all his classes that he wouldn't be back after the break, that someone named Mr. Smiley would be taking the class on a permanent basis.

Someone in Beth's class — not Beth, who was not about to give him the satisfaction of

148

a visible reaction — expressed surprise at this.

"But I thought it was always clear that I was just filling in until the school could get someone permanent," he said. "I've been working on a novel for a year now and want to get back to it before I forget the names of my characters. But it's been a very good time for me here at Hamilton. I don't think I'll ever forget any of you."

Well, I'll do my best to forget you, Beth thought, stung that he had never mentioned his leaving to her, nor ever told her — in all their conversations about writing — that he was a writer himself. Clearly nothing had been going on with him. She had been a fool.

Which was how she still felt the night of the dance, watching him from across the dance floor as he kidded around with the other teachers. As the night wore on, she could see different girls asking him to dance. Which he did, and quite well from what she could see, although always in a formal way, holding them far away from himself, as if they were large, melting ice cubes.

Beth would never give him the satisfaction of asking him to dance, although she longed — in spite of herself — to be one of the melting ice cubes. He nodded and smiled at her several times as he danced past the punch table during the course of the evening. Each time she managed to look fast in another direction so as not to have to look back at him.

Around ten-thirty, they ran out of punch

and had only broken cookies left, and Lorraine decided it was probably late enough to fold up the refreshments.

"If they get thirsty from now on, they can go out to the drinking fountain," she told Beth.

Later on, thinking the evening over, Beth figured out that he must have been watching her pretty closely because, right in the minute or so between when she finished cleaning up the punch table — rinsing out the bowl, crumpling up the glitter-sprinkled white crepe paper tablecloth and tossing it in the waste basket, eating two of the cookie chards left on the platter and dumping the rest — and the moment when she was going to go and get her coat and leave, he came up from behind her.

"All the other girls asked me to dance," he said in a low voice spoken very close to her ear. "One of the fringe benefits of being a teacher. But I get the feeling you're not going to ask me."

She didn't turn around.

"You've got it right," she said.

"Then I'll have to make the advances." He came around in front of her, gave a little half-bow like a member of some eighteenth-century European court and said, "May I — that is if your card isn't filled — may I have this dance?"

If he had given her a chance, she might have said no, but it wasn't a real question, followed immediately, as it was, by his arm slipping around her waist and a quick spin out onto the floor.

He did not hold her like she was a melting block of ice.

He was a wonderful dancer. She could close her eyes and let him do all the guiding. When she opened them, the gym, she had to admit — although mercifully not out loud this time — did look not unlike a winter wonderland.

He didn't say anything during the whole number. When it was over, he pulled back from her and said, very seriously, "I don't think it would do for me to dance more than one dance with you, but if you would care to meet me in five minutes in my classroom, I have something I'd like to say to you."

And then he was gone, walking across the floor toward a small clump of teachers, asking old Mrs. Wiggie to dance.

Beth went to the girls' room, combed her hair, splashed water on her face to quiet the red down, and took a slow walk to the stairwell and up to Room 205.

It seemed a lot longer than five minutes waiting there in the classroom — strange in its darkness, familiar in its smells of floor wax and chalk dust.

She tried to guess what Evans might say. As usual, he had her at a disadvantage. She had wanted a showdown, but because he had called it, she was caught unprepared. She was flustered and he wasn't even there yet.

And then he *was* there, preceded by a long minute of his heels hitting the old tile floors of the hall.

"Hi," he said, casually, as if they had just run into each other accidentally in front of the library on Maple Avenue.

"Hi." Two could play this game, she thought. It's his showdown. Let him go through the awkward part of getting into it.

"Oh, my," he said, sighing and letting himself fall backward against the wall next to Beth. "I feel like I'm seventeen."

"Awful, isn't it," she said.

They both laughed. When they stopped he said, "There's a couple of parts to what I have to say. One is that I'm not a complete dope. I know what's been going on. What I mean is that I've been aware for a while of your feelings for me."

"I thought maybe you were, but I couldn't tell."

"That was probably because I was trying not to acknowledge them. I guess I hoped if I ignored them, they'd go away."

"Oh," she said.

"Please wait. I can hear the hurt in your voice. You have to hear the other part. It's that your feelings were partly reciprocated. You have become special to me. As a student, but also as a person. I see qualities in you that impress me."

"This sounds like you're hiring me for a job."

"Well, I'm trying to keep this as abstract

as possible. You want me to get it down to the nitty gritty?"

"Please," she heard herself say.

"I'm not going to fall in love with you."

"Oh."

"I probably could, but I'm not going to let myself. I'm not all that generous a guy, but I'm being a real sport with you. You're at this terrific place, the end of your senior year coming up, then the last summer of freedom before everyone starts expecting you to act like an adult. Then college, which is going to open all the windows of your mind and blow hurricanes through them. And this is all stuff you have to go through alone, or with other people who are sharing the experience. I've already been there. I'm somewhere else now and I don't want to tie you up with me. It would cheat you of finding yourself. You know, this happens all the time. Two people meet and they're right, but the time is wrong. That's all it is with us. Our timing's off."

"But . . ."

"No," he said, softly but firmly. "No buts."

"We'd better get back," he said after a small silence had fallen between them. "Do you think we could wish each other well and shake on it?"

"Do you think," she asked, "we could wish each other well and kiss on it?"

"I guess we could risk that," he said. She couldn't see his face in the dark, but thought, from the sound of his voice, that he was smiling at her audacity.

They were still shoulder to shoulder, leaning against the wall. He turned around to face her, putting one hand up against the bulletin board behind her, the other lightly on her shoulder. He leaned in and kissed her. On the lips, but very, very softly. A phantom kiss. And then he was gone.

She stood there a while, absorbing the experience, prolonging the moment, not knowing whether to feel happy or sad.

Eventually, she heard people-leaving noises from down the hall. The dance was apparently over. She would have to leave or risk getting locked in. Reluctantly, she walked down to the cloak room, got her coat, and walked out into the still, mild, winter night.

She hadn't been walking long — she had just turned onto Main — when she heard a low, automotive rumbling behind, then alongside her. She stopped and turned to see a taxi pulling up at the curb. The driver leaned across the front seat, threw open the door on the passenger side, and beckoned her over with a wave of his hand.

At first she was startled and a little frightened. Then she saw the red hair and began to laugh.

"Wanna ride, lady?" Rick asked. "For you I won't even turn on the meter."

"Not tonight," she said. "Tonight I've got some walking alone to do. But you could give me a call sometime."

"You know," he said, "I just might do that." He blew her a kiss before he pulled away.

The walk home was a short one, but by the time she turned the corner onto her block, she had already decided that Evans was probably right. It looked like there were going to be at least a few interesting times ahead.